Penumbra

by

Thomas Fenske

Penumbra

"It's Holly. Earl just called me and put Dave on the phone."

"What? He's okay?"

"He told me he was with Earl and Ding and he begged me to bring the paper to them. Alone. Otherwise they're going to kill him."

"Oh, dear. You're not going to do it, are you?"

"He said I don't have any other choice."

"Listen, if a man gives you just one choice, you have to figure out the other options he doesn't want you to think about. Either that or you need to consider possibilities he hasn't thought of yet. Where was he calling from?"

"He said they were near Carlsbad...they want to meet me in the parking lot of a store on the west side of town, on Lea Street. I need to be there at 5 tomorrow morning with that paper."

"Carlsbad ain't too far, but Sam has the paper and he's still not here."

Holly's voice trembled, "Oh, dear."

"Anyway, you shouldn't go there alone. Let me see if I can talk to Lance or Mule so we can figure something out."

Holly sobbed lightly. "Okay."

After hanging up, she started looking for Mule's number, but the phone rang again.

"Smidgeon?"

"Sam! Where are you?"

"We just pulled into Carlsbad. Ximena made me stop and call you."

Smidgeon's heart skipped a beat. "What?"

"She suddenly pointed at a pay phone on the side of the road and said I needed to call you right away. Is there anything wrong?"

"I *just* got off the phone with Holly. She told me that Earl called and let her talk to Dave. *He's* in Carlsbad with Earl and Ding. She is supposed to go by herself along with the paper and meet them at a small store on Lea Street at 5 in the morning. She said it is on the west side of town."

"I have the paper."

"I know that. I was just fixing to call Mule to ask him what we should do when you called."

"Call Holly, and tell her to stay put. I'll handle it."

"Sam, how can you face off with Earl and Ding? You don't even have a gun."

"I have *Ximena*."

What They Are Saying About Penumbra

"This is the fourth book in the Traces of Treasures series, and, like the first three, it did not disappoint! Sam and Smidgeon, along with their friends, are at it again on the hunt for a treasure, but who's the true owner of the much sought after cache? Friendship and faith collide with evil as the mystery unravels in this page turning story."
—Marianne Reese, book blogger and author of
Skylar Moon https:\\mariannereeseauthor.wordpress.com

"Whose treasure is it? How can it be found? Who knows the secret to finding something buried centuries before? Who will live to uncover the truth? Who is scamming whom? Hang on tight, this down home mystery has Sam and company up to their pickaxes in deceit and the supernatural and you are going to love it as old friends return, once again"
—Diane Bylo, Tome Tender Book Blog
https://tometender.blogspot.com

"(Fenske) writes a tight, intriguing story set in the desert southwest—or as we know it, God's Country. His characters are contrary but honest, and his background and scenic descriptions are spot-on. The addition of mystical and possibly unhappy spirits is an added bonus. Mixed into *Penumbra* is a posse of good friends, conscientious law enforcement, polite, helpful people, and excellent food—I enjoyed that part of traveling back in the day. You will, too. And the bad guys are satisfyingly bad. Definitely a win-win novel."
—Bonnye Reed Fry, GoodReads reviewer.

Penumbra

by

Thomas Fenske

Adventure/Mystery Fiction Novel

Published by Thomas Fenske

Copyright © 2020 by: Thomas Fenske
ISBN: 979-8-9928799-3-3

Originally Published by Wings ePress, Inc.
Edited by: Jeanne Smith
Copy Edited by: Rebecca Smith
Executive Editor: Jeanne Smith
Cover Artist: Trisha FitzGerald-Jung

Published In the United States Of America

Dedication

I dedicate this book to all of my family: my wonderful wife, daughter, and sons; my sisters, my aunt, and all of my cousins.

Acknowledgments

I would like to thank Marianne Reese, Ginger Millican, and Janet Peri for reading early versions of this novel and offering valuable insight.

pe·num·bra

/pəˈnəmbrə/

noun -

-The partially shaded outer region of the shadow cast by an opaque object.

-The shadow cast by the earth or moon over an area experiencing a partial eclipse.

One

Sam winced against a searing pain shooting up his leg. He fought the spinning swirls in his vision he knew led to unconsciousness and crooked his head to the left at the sound of the car door creaking open.

"Hey! You okay?" The voice seemed to come from a foggy abyss.

Sam struggled to focus and made out the features of a stranger peering down at him, eyes widened with concern.

Sam panted but managed to blurt out, "I, I'm not sure...leg hurts."

A new face replaced the first. "Sorry, man, I messed up."

A woman's voice pierced the veil. "I saw the whole thing from my porch. He tried to pass you, but you were turning left. I've already called the police."

Sam blinked sweat out of his eyes and struggled to sort through the jumble of signals cartwheeling through his brain. He closed his eyes and some thoughts gradually came back into focus.

He remembered driving home, clicking his left blinker, and turning down his street. Then everything went black. He opened his eyes and again saw the hazy intersection visible on the other side of his cracked windshield. Several figures were milling around, and to Sam it seemed like a scene from a movie. He tried to shift his leg and grimaced again; he had momentarily forgotten the pain but it came back with a vengeance. Flashing lights punctuated the scene in a staccato of red and white.

"Somebody hit me?"

The first voice returned. "Yeah, looks like they knocked you into a mesquite tree, then your car bounced all the way around. You say your leg hurts?"

"Yeah...a lot. I, I don't think I can move."

"That's all right, buddy, you stay right there. Here's the cops."

Another face blurred into view. "You hurt? Sam? Sam?"

Sam had momentarily closed his eyes, but he recognized the voice of local sheriff's deputy Clay Dodge. He became aware of unmistakable odors, burned oil and antifreeze, but the antifreeze confused him since his Volkswagen had an air-cooled engine.

He snapped his eyes open again and was gratified to see Clay's familiar face. He'd always liked the deputy.

"Yeah. My leg's hurt bad. I must have put my foot on the brake when things started happening. I don't remember exactly. All I know is, I was driving, and now I'm here."

"I saw it all." It was the same woman he had heard earlier.

"Thank you, ma'am. I'll get your statement in a minute, but first I need to check on the ambulance."

Clay disappeared and Sam was vaguely aware of an array of faces peering in at him until Clay reappeared.

"Ambulance is almost here, Sam. I had dispatch call Smidgeon, too."

"She'll freak out to see me like this."

"Just take it easy, Sam, it'll be okay. We'll take good care of you. Did you hit your head?"

"I don't think so, but I'm just a little rattled anyway." He reached up to his shoulder. "Think the seat belt bruised me a little."

"Good thing you were wearing it. A bruise is nothing compared to what you get if you smash your head into the windshield."

Wailing sirens beyond his view pierced the murmur of voices. He heard a shriek, then a familiar voice.

"Sam!" He felt a wave of relief as Smidgeon's face materialized.

"It's okay, honey, I think I'm okay."

She glanced around at the onlookers. "Can't somebody help him?"

"We're waiting for the ambulance," Clay said. "Sam said his leg is hurting him, so the fire department is coming, too, in case he's trapped. The car isn't on fire, so it's best to let them check him before they start to pull him out."

More flashes of light rolled across his vision and the sirens abruptly stopped. He looked up and marveled at the continuing dance of red and white flickering across Smidgeon's face.

Smidgeon held his hand. "Help's here, baby."

He took a deep breath and sighed. "Okay." Even in his confused state, he knew the real pain was going to come when they pulled him out of the wreckage, and he was already trying to prepare himself for the onslaught.

A new uniformed figure came into his view. "Sir, we're here to help you. What's your name?"

"Sam Milton."

"Do you know where you are?"

"Down the street from my house in Van Horn."

"Where are you injured?"

"My leg for sure. I think the rest of me is okay."

He heard the sound of thick fabric being cut and realized they were cutting the seat belt strap. Hands gently felt around his head and neck.

"No pain here?"

"No, I think my shoulder is bruised and I'm a little rattled, but it's mostly my leg."

Hands gently probed down his legs.

"I don't think you're stuck in there and that's good, so we're going to try to swing your body out. It's probably going to hurt."

"I figured it might." He attempted to laugh but couldn't.

As much as he had tried to prepare himself beforehand, the searing agony in his leg multiplied as first two, then four people grabbed him and he was lifted out of the driver's seat. Sam was unaccustomed to being so easily manipulated by other people. He experienced a momentary floating sensation before he landed on something hard. A renewed thunderbolt of unbearable pain shot through his leg. The pain relaxed into a steady agony that rose and subsided with every heartbeat. He took another deep breath, looked to the side and saw Smidgeon looking down at him with tears streaming down her face.

"Don't worry, I'm in good hands," he said. Then he felt a pinprick and the throbbing began to taper off a little.

An unfamiliar voice said, "There, Sam, I gave you something for the pain."

He managed a meek, "Thanks."

4

"Get that leg stabilized, we need to take him on to Culberson."

The painkiller began to dull his senses as an efficient and practiced blur of activity stirred around him.

Clay appeared again. "I'll see you at the hospital, Sam. Got a good eyewitness and the other driver has been cooperative."

"Was it my fault?"

Clay laughed. "Not at all, don't worry about that. I've got you covered."

Smidgeon came back into focus. "I'm going to follow them to the hospital and I'll see you there. They say it's just a broken leg."

Sam closed his eyes again as he was whisked into the back of the ambulance. His mind was numbed by painkillers and he was content to let the people do their work. At the hospital, amid a dizzying list of questions, several others assured him he was going to be all right.

A nurse asked, "What's your birthday?"

"Nine, ten, fifty-two."

"Not good enough, I need the whole date, not just the year."

"Nine, ten, fifty-two."

He heard her sigh. A face neared and eyes peered into his as a hand held his eyelid. Even in his dreamlike state he understood the problem.

"September tenth, nineteen fifty-two...nine, ten, fifty-two."

The nurse laughed. "Oh, sorry, honey."

"Leave me alone. I don't feel good."

Shortly after an IV was inserted into his arm, he drifted into unconsciousness.

When he blinked awake again, Smidgeon was holding his hand and gazing at him.

"Thank heavens…I thought you'd never wake up."

"What time is it?"

"It's morning, a little after eight."

"Really? I've been out that long?"

She nodded. "Yep, you've been asleep all night. Are you thirsty? I've got a Coke here." She handed Sam her drink and he sucked on the straw.

"So glad Coke is back to normal. That so-called *new* Coke just wasn't as good. It was the biggest business mistake of 1985. Hey, what about the café?"

She laughed. "Now I know you're going to be okay. Don't worry. The café is open as usual. Lance is there, but he said he hoped you'd forgive his absence. He stayed here with me for a long time until I made him go home to get some sleep."

"So somebody hit me?"

"Yeah, some guy caught you in the middle of an intersection. I guess he decided to pass you just as you started your turn. He said there were four cars, you were the second and he was the fourth. He claimed he started passing before he saw your blinker. This was just down the street from our house. Your car is totaled."

"Yeah, typical Van Horn traffic jam," Sam quipped. "I remember the pickup in front of me was going slow, but I was coming up to our street so I wasn't too worried about it."

"The guy behind you verified you had your blinker on. Both he and the woman whose yard you landed in were witnesses. The truck hit your back fender and ricocheted you off a mesquite tree. His truck was stopped cold because it smashed in his radiator."

"It happened so fast, it sort of knocked me for a loop."

There was a tapping on the door and a tall smiling man in surgical scrubs came in.

"I'm Doctor Smythe," he said. "It seems you had quite an evening."

"Guess so. What's the word, Doc?"

"I've got good news and less good news—you broke the tibia in your left leg. That's the larger bone on the lower part of your leg. It's actually a pretty common injury in traffic accidents. The good news is it isn't a compound fracture."

"What's the less good news?"

"Well, there isn't an orthopedist here. We stabilized it, but you really need to see a specialist in El Paso."

Sam looked at Smidgeon.

"We'll do what we have to do, Sam."

"What if we just set it and put it in a cast?"

"I wouldn't advise that. I mean, it might heal, but it probably wouldn't, because the tibia absorbs a lot of stress and strain. It tends to re-break easily before it's healed. It would be better for a specialist to stabilize it, probably with a rod and screws. Rest assured they'll give you the best options for treatment. I'm sure you'll be back in the saddle in no time."

"Oh, so that's my best option?" Sam asked.

The doctor nodded. "More good news...we can make it stable enough for you to transport yourself. Except for a few bumps and bruises, this is your only injury. If you use crutches and are careful, you'll be mobile enough to make the trip. No need for an ambulance or anything like that."

Smidgeon said, "That *is* good news, honey."

"Well, I guess you're driving me to El Paso."

The doctor scribbled something and said, "I'll set up the referral. I'll tell them you need to be seen as soon as possible."

After Doctor Smythe left, Sam turned to Smidgeon. "How are we going to pay for this?"

"We've still got a bit of money saved, but seriously, this was a car accident that wasn't your fault. I've got the other driver's insurance information, so his insurance should pay."

"Oh, right."

"We'll do whatever we need to do, okay?"

"I know better than to argue with you."

Smidgeon bent over Sam and hugged and kissed him. "Glad to hear your training is going well. Now that I've got you, Sam Milton, I want to keep you healthy. You'd do the same for me, wouldn't you?"

"You know I would."

The doctor returned holding a sheet of paper. "I've set up an appointment for you at eleven tomorrow morning. I wanted to give you some travel time."

Smidgeon took the paper and glanced over the information. "I know right where this is. Thank you, Doctor."

"When can I be released?"

"As soon as we finish the paperwork. A nurse should be by with a wheelchair and a pair of crutches in just a few minutes." The doctor paused at the door. "Stay completely off that leg. That should be easy advice for you to follow because if you try to put any weight on it, the pain will remind you."

Sam swallowed. "I understand." After the doctor left he said to Smidgeon, "Crutches. I hate crutches."

"Everybody hates them, sweetie. You'll just have to toughen up and do what you have to do to get better."

When the nurse arrived with the wheelchair, she pushed Sam to the front door of the small hospital where Smidgeon was waiting with her car. They both helped him up and he tested the crutches.

"I'll need to adjust them a little when I get home."

He angled himself into the passenger seat and prepared for the pain of the drive home. He knew he was going to be intimately aware of every bump.

"Are you hungry?"

"Starving. I haven't eaten since yesterday."

"That's right...you arrived after supper and barely nibbled your breakfast. I'll stop at the café and grab us something. I need to touch base with Lance and, anyway, I know he's worried about you, too."

"What's the special today?"

"*Texicali Arroz Con Pollo.*"

"Great. I hope Lance has it ready. Some good comfort food will help soothe my aches and pains."

Smidgeon chuckled. "It's after eleven...he'd better have it ready or he'll have a bunch of angry customers."

Smidgeon parked out front and disappeared through the door. In a few minutes a throng of customers came out and approached the car.

"Sam, you get better, y'hear?"

"I was so worried when I heard you were in an accident, glad you're okay. I'll include you in my prayers."

"My brother had a broken leg like that...you'll be okay if you just do what the doctor says."

Sam was almost embarrassed by the attention, but he also appreciated the concern of these people he saw so often. Not that long ago, he'd been an outsider, but now he felt he was truly a part of the community.

Lance came out, waving to Sam as he walked up to the car. "You had me worried there, buddy, but Smidgeon said you'll be good as new in no time."

"Well, I hope so."

"Don't worry, I've got this, but I better get on with my cooking."

"As soon as I get settled at the house I'll make sure Smidgeon comes back."

"I can handle the place all right. She said she has to haul you to El Paso tomorrow. Don't be surprised if they keep you for a day or two."

"What? Why?"

"Don't forget, I used to play football. They like to screw up broken leg bones and that means surgery."

"Lordy, the doctor said something like that but I thought it was a last resort."

"We'll see, won't we?" Lance looked up. "Here comes Smidgeon with your food. I'll try to come by and yak some more with you tonight, okay?" Lance shook Sam's hand, hugged Smidgeon and headed back into the café. Smidgeon handed Sam two bags. One smelled of Mexican spices. He sniffed at the other and said, "What else did you get...pie?"

"Country Chocolate Chess Pie."

"I could get used to this luxury."

"You know I don't much like us eating up the profits, but today is special."

"We eat up the profits all the danged time," he said. Then the car hit a deep pothole and Sam winced. "But right this second, it doesn't feel quite so special."

"I know, honey, but let's just get through these next few days and everything will get back to normal."

Two

The mid-afternoon sun blazed through the doorway and a woman entered and hesitated as her eyes adjusted to the more moderate light inside the cafe. The woman smiled when she caught Smidgeon's gaze and walked over. Smidgeon had glanced at her when she entered and, at first impression, she thought the face was familiar but couldn't quite place her. She knew just about everyone in town, but random travelers were frequent visitors.

"Just sit anywhere you want."

The woman sat at the nearest table and said, "You were right, this place really *is* just like the other café."

"Excuse me? I'm sorry, have we met?"

"Yes, several months ago up in Roswell."

A rush of memories flooded Smidgeon's mind. "Roswell! I knew you looked familiar..." she paused, searching for a name amidst the swirl of thoughts.

The woman smiled and extended a hand. "Holly."

"Holly, of course. You were my waitress when I stopped for a bite to eat, and you helped me figure out a goofy word puzzle I was struggling with. How'd you find your way here?"

"You gave me your card, remember? I was nearby and I realized the town sounded familiar. I looked in my purse and found I still had the card stuffed in there. How'd that puzzle work out for you?"

"It helped, it definitely helped. You just passing through?"

"Maybe. I'm not sure. I'm looking for my boyfriend. He's missing. Can we talk?"

"Let me get you a menu."

"Just a cup of coffee."

"I'll get two...let's move over to the corner table. It's the best I can do for a little privacy."

Smidgeon returned with two cups of coffee and sat across from Holly. She gave the newcomer a quick once-over. Her clothes were rumpled and her hair was a mess. Her makeup was fading and there were smudges where she'd unsuccessfully tried to wipe away the streaks of mascara that indicated she'd recently done her share of crying. Holly's gaze met Smidgeon's as they both took a first tentative sip.

"Good coffee," Holly said.

"It's pretty fresh." Smidgeon then got down to business. "So, what's troubling you? If I were to guess, I'd say it has to do with that boyfriend."

"Well..." Holly began, then her eyes moistened. "There's more to it than that. I confess, I came here because you, well, I had a hunch you could help me."

"Me? Why would you think that? We talked for about five minutes."

"Oh, not with the relationship; it goes way beyond that. I thought maybe you'd been involved in this sort of thing before. I mean treasure...nobody has clues like you had if they aren't looking for some kind of treasure, am I right?"

Smidgeon took a sip of coffee and never took her eyes off Holly. "That's a good guess. Seriously. I've had more than my fair share of such doings. Why don't you tell me what's going on."

The café door opened again and a tall gentleman walked in and waved to Smidgeon.

"Hey, Mule. You're running late today."

"An old man should be able to sleep in every now and then."

Smidgeon pointed to the chair next to hers, "Come on over and take a load off."

Holly had a puzzled look on her face.

"Don't worry, I just have an inkling he's someone you'll want to meet."

"Ladies? I don't believe I've had the pleasure," Mule said, extending his hand. "Mule Hollis."

"Holly Slidell."

As Mule settled his large frame into the chair, Smidgeon said, "Holly here has some troubles and was just about to tell me what's going on."

A look of shock crossed Holly's face, and Smidgeon added, "Mule here is a private investigator. He sort of stations himself here in the café most days."

He laughed. "Well, I haven't hung out a shingle or anything, but why don't you tell me what's troubling you?"

Holly stared at the steam rising out of her mug and took a deep breath. "My boyfriend has been missing for about a month."

"Are you sure he's missing? I mean, could he have maybe decided to leave you and forgot to mention it?" Mule asked.

Holly blinked back at him. "Why would you say that?"

"It's just that I've seen that sort of thing before. Okay, so how was your relationship?"

"Things had actually been pretty good between us, but he got wind of some kind of lost treasure and like a fool, he took off after it. He said he'd probably be gone a couple of weeks or so, but to come looking for him if he was any longer. After three weeks, I pulled all my money out of the bank and left my job."

Smidgeon reached out and took Holly's hand in hers. "Roswell is pretty far away. Do you think he went as far as Texas?"

"He said it was likely over north of Las Cruces, but beyond that he was vague. I've been driving around hoping I'd see his truck. I've asked about lost treasures here and there but most people just laugh. It seems like there's some kind of story about lost treasure everywhere you turn."

The door opened again and Holly said, "You're busy. I think I'm just wasting your time."

Smidgeon glanced behind her. "That's just my boyfriend Sam and our friend Lance. They both work here but they've been over in El Paso."

Sam struggled into the café brandishing a pair of crutches.

"Over here, honey."

Sam and Lance sat at the next table. "What's going on?" Sam asked.

"I don't know about all of this," Holly said, as she began to rise, but Smidgeon grasped her forearm.

"Just give it a second, sweetie. What was it you told me in Roswell about how a second set of eyes can help?" Smidgeon waved her arm at Mule, Lance, and Sam. "Listen, all of us know more about this kind of thing than you can even imagine, so now you've got a second, third, fourth, and fifth set of eyes."

"Maybe you're right."

"Darn tooting I'm right. Now, before we get back to business," she turned toward Sam, "what did the doctor in El Paso say?"

"Tibia's healing well, but I've still got a bit of time off my leg."

"That's okay, you can still work the register."

Sam chuckled. "Great. So what's going on?"

Mule responded, "Miss Holly here is in some trouble and was just about to tell us about it. Something about lost treasure." He pointed at Sam. "Sam and Lance here are our resident experts on lost treasure, so maybe you've come to the right place."

Sam held up his palms. "Hey, I just work here."

"Dang, let the lady talk. Oh, I'm sorry, I'm Lance," he said, standing and shaking Holly's hand.

"Pleased to meet you. Well, I guess I should start over. My boyfriend is missing. He said he was following a hunch he'd heard about a lost treasure, somewhere over north of Las Cruces."

"That's pretty far from here."

"Yes, but I didn't know where else I could go. I've been driving around, looking in wider and wider circles but found no trace of him or his truck. I didn't even find much of anything about any lost treasure he might be looking for. I was at a loss of where to turn next. Then I remembered Smidgeon."

Smidgeon turned to Sam. "Holly's the waitress I told you about."

"Oh, I remember. She helped you out when you were on the road."

Holly resumed, "I don't know about all of that, but I never forgot you." She squeezed Smidgeon's hand. "I don't know...I had a feeling you might be able to help."

Mule laughed as he pointed around the small group. "I reckon this a bit more than you bargained for."

Sam said, "I've done a lot of research on local treasures. Do you know anything else that might be a clue of what he was looking for?"

"All he called it was Archangel. Nobody I talked to had ever heard of anything like that."

Sam whistled under his breath. "The Archangel Cache."

"You know it?" Lance asked.

"I saw it in a book when I was looking for information on *our* mine."

Holly blinked in surprise. "Excuse me, *your* mine?"

Lance laughed. "We had a bit of tension with a different treasure a while back, but it's a story for another time. We need to concentrate on your problem."

Holly looked at Sam. "What do you know about the...what did you call it?"

"Well, the full name is the Saint Michael the Archangel Cache. It's just one of the dozens of lost treasure stories told throughout west Texas and New Mexico. I don't know much, but I remember a small entry in one book I read. Supposedly, a caravan was carrying gold and silver back to Mexico from the Santa Fe area when they were ambushed by raiders. According to the legend, a cache of treasure was hidden before they were slaughtered. Well, one soldier survived and managed to find his way to help, but his ordeal left him unable to remember precisely where the cache was buried."

"When was this supposed to have happened?" Mule asked.

"Sometime in the 1700s."

Lance said, "Almost three hundred years is a long time."

"There are a lot of stories like that," Sam said. "What made your boyfriend think he had a solid lead?"

"Dave, his name is Dave. I'm not sure. Some guys he met in a bar told him about it...at least I think that's where he heard about it."

Lance scratched the back of his head. "Oh, Lordy, he gallivanted off to look for a treasure he heard about from some drunks in a bar? Did he go off with them?"

"No, I don't think so. I'm pretty sure he took off on his own."

Mule tapped the table with meaty fingers. "Ma'am, I don't want to pry none, but I've made a pretty good business off stuff like this. You sure he didn't just leave you? I mean, could it be he got tired of the relationship and decided to go off and start plowing in another field? Frankly this sounds a lot like that."

Tears began to well in Holly's eyes. "Maybe, but in my heart I don't think so. We were doing okay. I know it sounds silly, but I think he wanted to strike it rich so we could get married. We were making it, just not getting ahead. No, I think he was looking for easy money."

"Ain't no easy money in hunting for lost treasure," Sam said. "Been there, done that. But I do understand the obsession with the idea of it. Had a buddy who called it 'The Fever.' He told me, 'it's whatever gets under your skin and makes you scratch the ground looking to get rich.' I had it pretty bad, so I know."

"You did?"

Smidgeon nodded. "Yes, he did."

"Yeah, long story. I should write a book. So if you knew to focus near Las Cruces, why did you come here? We're pretty far from there. How'd you even find Smidgeon?"

Smidgeon pointed at Holly. "That day she helped me with the word puzzle, I gave her my card."

Mule spoke up. "I've heard enough. I'll see what I can do to help you, young lady."

"I can't afford to pay. Well, pay much. I'm just about out of money."

Smidgeon spoke up. "I can help, too. I know you're a good waitress, why don't you work here? I'll front you a little cash to keep you going until you start earning your keep."

"I'd say she could stay with us, but Mule is using the third bedroom for an office," Lance said.

"I know the new owners of Dolings Motel, I'm sure we can get you set up over there. It's close to here. Don't judge this place by the mid-afternoon...mornings and lunch are real busy and weekends are steady. I've been thinking about putting on somebody anyway, especially with Sam being hurt."

Mule pulled out a small notebook. "First things first. What's Dave's last name?"

"Adams. His full name is David Adams."

"What was he driving?"

"A rusty white Dodge pickup, 1975, I think."

"Okay, that's a start. I'll see what I can find regarding his name and the vehicle description. Sam, do you think you can dig up anything more on this...what was it called?"

"The Saint Michael the Archangel Cache."

"Dave just called it Archangel."

"Yeah, the whole name is a mouthful. Of course, I'm limited in what I can do with being laid up," Sam said, slapping his leg.

"I can help you," Lance said.

"And so can I," Smidgeon said.

"I do need to go back to El Paso next week for some X-rays. There was a problem today and they couldn't take them."

Smidgeon asked, "Can't you get them here?"

"Doc doesn't trust them, so he wants me to do it there, but their machine was down today. The good news is we can maybe drop by the university library while we're in town."

"Oh, good idea. I hadn't even thought of that. Our tiny library wouldn't have anything you could use."

Sam shook his head. "I doubt it."

Holly sat with her hands folded, looking at the four people surrounding her. "I don't know what to say."

Smidgeon stood. "How about 'all right, then?'"

"What's a man have to do to get a bite to eat around here?" Mule asked.

Smidgeon pulled out her pad and pen, but Holly reached out and took them. "I guess if I'm going to work here, I better get started. Do you know what you want?"

"DTD, fries, and coffee."

"Just write it down, the cook knows that means Double Trouble Dog. I'll bring you up to speed on our menu."

"Double Trouble Dog." Holly giggled. "Okay." She handed the pad back to Smidgeon. "You guys just sort of jumped into my dilemma, so I thought it best I start repaying the favor."

"We'll do our best to take care of you, sweetie. You want a DTD, too? It's probably a good idea for you to eat before we get you situated over at the motel."

"Yes, that would be great. Uh, what is the DTD? Did you say Double Trouble Dog?"

"Let's fix you one first. I know you'll like it and you won't get anything like it anyplace else."

Sam made his way over to the register. "I better get to work."

"What happened to you?" Holly asked.

"Car wreck, broke a bone in my leg. I'll be okay."

Mule said, "After I eat, I'll head to my office and call some people I know. Might ask the local cops, too. Maybe Clay Dodge can check his police alerts for me."

Three

Mule was working at his small desk when he heard the faint rumbling of a truck outside. He looked up at a nearby clock.

"Right on time."

Mule walked into the hallway and saw that Lance's dog was already wagging her tail by the door. She let out a welcoming yip as the door opened and Lance entered carrying a bag.

"Honey, I'm home," he quipped before bending over to rub the dog's head. "I'm glad to see you, too, Prewash."

Mule took the bag and turned to take it into the kitchen. "That's getting so old it's not funny anymore. So what's for dinner tonight? I figure it's either a leftover of today's special or it's a hamburger, right?"

"Yeah, today's special was our chicken casserole. You know, if you're getting tired of the free food, you could cook something different if you want. I mean, we could be doing a lot worse."

Mule turned, showing a big grin. "It *would* be a lot worse if I cooked. I promise you that. Anyway, I like the chicken casserole."

"Me, too. I'll get some plates."

"Lance, I have to admit, I was skeptical when you offered me a room in your house. I'm a bit of an old dog and didn't think I'd take to having a roommate."

"Hey, it's Sam's house, not mine, but when you said you were thinking about setting up shop here instead of Colorado City, I figured I might as well make use of these extra bedrooms.

"Got me my own phone line and one of those fancy answering machines. Takes the strain off my daughter-in-law. With another baby coming, she didn't need to be worrying about my business."

Mule divvied the casserole between two plates as Lance got the silverware and two beers from the refrigerator. They carried their bounty to the small table and sat, where they momentarily bowed their heads before Mule said grace.

"Lord, make us truly thankful for these and all other blessings. In Jesus' name, amen."

Lance spread a napkin in his lap. "This is another reason why I like having you here. I'd let myself get out of the habit, but you never miss saying grace for us."

"My wife insisted and it just stuck with me. I guess it helps to remind me that she's still a part of me."

As they ate, Lance decided to broach the subject of the missing man. "So, did you get started on Holly's boyfriend?"

"I made a few calls, but haven't heard anything back yet. She's lucky I'm in a slack period. I don't reckon there's money to be made in this case, but I figured at the time this would be *pro bono* because I feel sorry for the poor woman."

"She does seem to have reached the end of her rope, emotionally and financially. We've all been there, I guess."

A phone rang down the hall and Mule hurried to answer it. Lance could hear some murmuring before his friend returned.

"A truck registered to David Adams was found abandoned near a place called Arabela in New Mexico. Buddy of mine works for the New Mexico state police, and he said it was reported to them a couple of weeks ago."

"Where the heck is Arabela?"

"I asked him the same thing. He said it's up near the Capitan Mountains and that it was a rugged area a bit out of the way. It's a start."

"Have they been investigating it?"

"Nothing much for them to investigate. I guess Holly never filed a missing person report. An abandoned vehicle is suspicious, but in and of itself is no indication of a crime. Sometimes a car breaks down and people figure it's the last straw, so they just leave it. They figure the state or county will pick it up and junk it for them. Most of the time they do."

"Yeah, I had a buddy who did that once when I was in college. I told him he was crazy but he just didn't want to deal with it anymore. He left it in a parking lot in the middle of Houston."

"The locals *did* think something was odd about it, though."

"What's that?"

"The keys were in it. They tried the ignition and it started right up; it even had a half tank of gas."

"So he didn't break down and he didn't run out of gas."

"Nope. It was on a trail just off a graded road that led to a place called Las Palas. A hunter found it parked under a tree."

"That's quite a bit of info."

"Yeah, and almost none of it is of much use."

Lance mused, "Except I guess it is a place to start looking."

Mule laughed out loud. "I'll make an investigator out of you yet."

"So, what's next?"

"Nothing to do but go out there and ask a few questions. Anything else would be hard because I can't go rambling off cross-country. These old knees of mine don't do rough trails so good anymore."

"I could do that part."

Mule huffed. "You?"

"Why not? Holly's almost up to speed at the café...she's got a lot of experience so she's been a fast study. I'm sure Smidgeon could spare me for a few days. We've been bouncing around duties a bit, but Sam can handle the register and Holly is doing great, so things are starting to smooth out."

"I thought you needed to haul Sam to El Paso next week."

"We haven't told Smidgeon yet, but he drove my truck on the way back, so I figure he can likely drive himself if he's driving an automatic. He's handling the crutches well, and he's been mindful of that leg."

Mule finished chewing another bit of food. "He was going to do some research on that Archangel thing when he was there, too."

Lance waved his hand in dismissal. "Again, he doesn't need me for that. Sam knows his way around a library."

"Well, let's make sure everything is good with him and Smidgeon before you commit. Anyway, that's next week. I was thinking of leaving maybe tomorrow or the next day. With a missing person, the trail gets colder every day you wait, and we've already got a late start on this."

Lance cleared the table while Mule retrieved a couple of maps from his office. He spread them on the table and they both concentrated on the locations and distances.

"Looks like it'll take maybe four or five hours to get there," Lance said.

Mule tapped his fingers while he contemplated the map. "I think you're right on the money. Not a fast trip, but not a long one either." He traced a line to the west. "Looks like he must have been heading west from where he left his truck." He traced a little further. "Capitan is a bigger town. Might serve as a base for more extensive work."

"Shouldn't we wait for Sam to do his research?"

"Dave could be in danger. Every day we wait might make it worse."

"Maybe we should get Holly to file a missing person report, get the authorities on it."

"To tell you the truth, I'm surprised she hasn't done that already. Maybe I should go see her. I'll call the motel and see if she'll talk to me. She probably knows more than she thinks she does."

Mule returned to his office and called the Dolings Motel. Shortly, Mule recognized Holly's voice.

"Holly, this is Mule Hollis. I've got some information on your boyfriend, David."

"Oh, you've started already? I didn't expect anything quite so fast. What is it?"

"I'd prefer to talk to you in person. Would it be all right if I dropped by? Sorry it's so late, but I'm close by and I do much better in person than I do on the phone."

"I'm too keyed up to sleep anyway, so I think it will be all right."

"Okay. I'll see you in a few minutes."

Mule hung up and grabbed his keys. He knew he could have just as easily talked on the phone, but in his line of work, it always seemed to work better for him if he asked questions in person so he could note any reactions. The eyes of a person were windows to their souls.

"Heading over there?"

"Yeah, she said it was okay."

"Want me to tag along?"

"Seriously, this sort of thing works better if it's one-on-one. I have a hunch she hasn't quite told us everything she knows. The best way for me to figure that out is to gauge her reactions to my direct questions."

Lance laughed, shaking his head. "So you want to use your cop sixth sense."

"Ex-cop," Mule reminded him.

"If it was out of your blood, you'd be laying bricks or working in a store, not private investigating."

Mule laughed. "I think you may be onto something there, pardner."

~ * ~

Mule pulled behind the motel and scanned the room numbers for the one Holly had given him. His experience in law enforcement had taught him several ways to knock on a door. These ranged from gentle tapping to hammering with a fist. In this case, there was no cause for alarm, so he approached the door and tapped gently.

Holly opened the door a crack and peeked out, then opened it wider. "Come in, Mr. Hollis."

Mule removed his Stetson and stepped across the threshold. A hint of perfume hung in the air. "Sit down," she said, indicating a chair already pulled away from the small table. She sat on the edge of the bed. He detected a faint aroma of alcohol on her breath and thought her makeup looked fresh.

"Smidgeon called you Mule...that's an unusual name."

"My given name is Mulvihill. It's a family name. Kids stumbled over it and took to calling me Mule. Nowadays, most people say it sort of fits my personality."

"So, you said you have news?"

"David's truck was found near a small town called Arabela. The keys were in it, it had plenty of gas, and it was operational."

"Operational? What does that mean?"

"It would start, which likely means he didn't break down. Did he have any family or acquaintances in that area?"

Holly blinked at him. He noted some scattered items on the counter by the sink, which confirmed what he had already observed about her makeup.

"Not that I know of."

"You said he was following a hunch. Any clue where he got that idea?"

"Dave went down to a local watering hole every Wednesday night. He took advantage of the fact that I always worked a double shift on Wednesdays. One night he came home pretty well blitzed, spouting a lot of nonsense about this Archangel thing. After that night it was all Dave could talk about. I think Sam was right about that fever thing."

"And how long has he been missing?"

"It's going on four weeks. He said to not worry unless he was gone more than two. He also told me not to call the police."

"Which is why you haven't filed him as a missing person."

"Right. I just left and started looking."

"But you didn't know to go find his truck...you never made it up to Arabela."

"I've never heard of that place."

While she talked, Holly's eyes almost never locked on Mule's steady gaze. To him that was a dead giveaway that she was holding back something.

"You sure about that? And why wouldn't he want you to call the police?"

"Are you really a private investigator? You sound more like a cop."

"Used to be a cop, now I'm doing my own thing. Look, if you want me to find Dave, you're going to have be one hundred percent honest with me."

She reached out and put her hand on Mule's arm, and gently squeezed. "What makes you think I'm not being honest?"

He moved his arm away from her hand. "That, for one. And you freshened your makeup, and I smell perfume and alcohol. I've been investigating long enough to know those aren't the signs a woman is too darned worried about her missing boyfriend."

She turned to the side and stifled a sob. "I'm sorry but, well, when you wanted to come over so late maybe I got the wrong impression. I'm not too ashamed to admit that I'm frustrated and lonely, but please understand, I really do miss him and I'm worried about him."

Mule stood. "You did get the wrong impression, but no matter. I understand. I was ready to head out and start tracking him. Every day is another day the trail gets colder. But now I'm not so sure any of this is a good idea. Whatever you thought might happen ain't going to happen, not with me. Paying or not paying, you are a client to me, that's all, and I know you haven't been totally honest with me. What are you not telling me?"

Holly began crying. "He's an ex-con on parole, okay? The people he met in the bar are friends of his from prison. This whole thing is based on some crazy stories they heard in jail. But then he took off on his own and never came back."

"So, if he was consorting with some cronies from the joint, it was a violation of his parole. Does his parole officer even know he's missing?"

"I don't know. I think he last checked in right before he left. Anyway, I know that's why he didn't want me going to the police."

"So, like most ex-cons, he's just looking for a way to make easy money. It could be he figured he was already in over his head and just headed out of town. It would be a way of protecting you both."

"I think he would have taken me with him. And the truck is proof that he was probably looking for the treasure, isn't it?

Mule stood at the door. "Yes, I'd say that it does."

"Then will you still help find him?"

"Yes, I'll help you find him. It's what I do, Miss Holly."

Four

Sam had just closed the cafe and he was working the register when he thought he heard a sound. He paused and looked up from the stacks of cash in front of him. Then he heard it again, a distinct tapping at the door. He grabbed his crutches, and as he approached the source, he saw the face of Mule Hollis. He reached up and turned the key he always left in the lock when he closed.

Sam let Mule in, locking the door behind him. "What's up?"

"I figured either you or Miss Smidgeon would be here. Sorry to get you onto your sore leg."

"No problem, I'm getting around pretty good on these things. Sorry, if you're hungry, the kitchen's shut down."

"No, I just wanted to run something past you, something I found out about Holly and her boyfriend. Come on, let's sit down over yonder, and get you off your good leg."

"Thanks." Sam pivoted over to the nearest table and sat down heavily. "Yeah, I get along okay, but I'll be glad when I can get back to normal. So what's up?"

"Well, last night she admitted to me that her boyfriend is an ex-con and his little expedition is related to some prison-related gossip. It turns out the people who told him about this Archangel thing were some of his recently released prison buddies."

"Interesting. And this concerns you?"

"Heck yeah. Anything con-related sort of perks my ex-cop ears up, but that ain't all. Once I got that information, I made a few more calls and got some of my contacts to dig a little deeper for me."

"And?"

"Her name is Holly, but it's not Slidell and she's got a record or her own, with petty theft charges all over New Mexico. She did a stretch, too, six months. Her name's Holly Marie Shankston. I thought you'd want to know."

"Oh, you're afraid she might have come here and wheedled her way in to rip us off?"

"It's a logical assumption, Sam, since it looks like most of her crimes involved employers."

"She have any open warrants?"

"Surprisingly, no. After her last conviction, she paid restitution in the remaining cases. I figure it was some sort of shock probation which is meant to enhance the inclination to go straight and narrow."

"You know, Smidgeon called the last place she worked."

"That gal doesn't miss a trick."

"No, she doesn't. The Roswell place said although she left in a hurry, it was on good terms. They said they would have no problem hiring her again if she came back. "

"Well, that sounds promising, but anyway, I thought you ought to know."

"I appreciate it. I'll tell Smidgeon and see if she wants to talk to Holly about it. Any news on the boyfriend? Lance said they found his truck."

"That's about it. The truck was abandoned out in the middle of nowhere. I'm fixing to head up there to nose around."

"Lance said he might be tagging along. We're still figuring out scheduling stuff."

"I guess two heads are sometimes better than one, and he has a good head on his shoulders."

"Lance is..." Sam hesitated, "Well, he's saved me more than once. He's almost family to me now."

"I know how that is, I'm kind of feeling the same way. Anyhow, I'm planning to head up there day after tomorrow. It'll just be a quick trip to talk to the locals and see if I can dig up any more info. Well, guess I'll leave you to it."

Mule stood and helped Sam to his feet. "Thanks. This is the part that gets a little tedious."

"I reckon."

Mule turned back toward Sam when they reached the door and added, "It's pretty spooky in here in the dark, you be careful, okay? Take care, Sam, I'll see you later."

"I always am," Sam said as he closed the door and hobbled back to the register.

He was finalizing his count when he heard his keys clink faintly as the door lock clicked. He looked up but could only see a hazy, fading glow, then a wispy apparition materialized.

"You didn't lock the door."

He squinted in the dim light and could barely make out familiar features of the face he saw looking at him.

"Loot, you scare the daylights out of me every time you do that!"

"Got to get your attention somehow. Every time I start to think I should be moving on, you somehow keep pulling me back. Your leg any better?"

"A little. It's a slow heal."

"Knew a cowboy who broke his shinbone one time when he got thrown by a horse. Seemed to take him forever to git back in shape. You know, you're a danged fool to leave that door unlocked when you've got cash out in the open like that."

"I know. Thanks."

"So, what's this latest thing you've gotten yourself into? Who's this woman? Something don't feel quite right to me, Sam."

"Smidgeon ran into her a while back…" Sam related the rest of what he knew.

"Hah. Treasure and trouble both seem to follow you around like a bunch of hound dog puppies."

Sam said, "That doesn't have anything to do with you hanging around me, does it?"

"I think it's related, but there isn't much I can do in this state either. I can feel myself already pulling away."

"Thanks for finally showing yourself. I'd missed our talks."

"Me, too. I'll come back as soon as I can, so's I can fill you in with anything I see."

As the apparition faded, Sam realized his muscles had tensed during the meeting and his heart was pounding. He took a deep breath and blew it out through his mouth.

"Still not used to him popping in like that," he said to himself. "I like knowing he is still around in his own way, but it is disturbing at the same time."

He thought back to his first night in the hospital after his surgery. He remembered waking up and seeing Smidgeon in a recliner beside him, snoring softly, but he became aware of an eerie glow on the other side and, to his astonishment, the glow settled into an image of Loot leaning over him, softly whispering, "Go back to sleep. You're going to be okay."

The next day, he wondered if perhaps it had been a dream, but it happened again a few days later at home. He had fallen asleep on the couch and MamaKat hissed, waking him up. He and Loot had a brief conversation about his accident, and Loot faded from view, promising he'd be back when he could.

"It explains quite a few things," Sam said out loud.

He'd long had a feeling he was being watched, especially when he used to hike alone in the desert. Sometimes the hair on the back of his neck would bristle and he'd feel as if something or someone was watching him, even before Loot passed away.

He mentioned this to Loot, who said, "I think Slim followed you for a while. And sometimes Lance's granddad Scamp has joined in, too." It was Slim who had first put Sam on the trail of lost gold. Lance's grandfather had done the same thing to *him*.

Sam said, "I saw you another time, too."

"Yep, managed to stop that fella in his tracks so's you could catch him."

Sam laughed. "I think seeing you drove him mad."

"Well, truth be told, I think he had a pretty good head start on that already."

Smidgeon and Mule had also seen the apparition that day, but they had never mentioned it again. Sam couldn't blame them. It was probably for the same reason he was content to keep these latest visitations to himself.

~ * ~

Smidgeon blew a stray strand of hair out of her eyes. "So Holly has a record? The café in Roswell said she was one of the best employees they'd ever had."

Sam adjusted himself on his stool behind the register. "And she seems fine. Maybe she's turned over a new leaf. It's just something Mule turned up, and he thought we ought to know about it."

"What does he think?"

"He's suspicious of anybody who lies."

"Well, she hasn't strictly lied about anything."

"Her name isn't Slidell, it's Shankston."

"I'm sure there is some explanation. I like Holly. I liked her when I first met her, too. I'll talk to her when she comes in. She's been doing really well here, and we're going to need her if Lance takes off with Mule."

"Yeah, he'll stay if he doesn't think we can handle things without him, but I know he really wants to go."

"He's worked for months without more than a day off here and there. It will do him good to get out and do something else, even for a few days. We'll just have to deal with it. You're okay where you are, but I worry about you being stuck just sitting there all day."

"Oh, I'm fine. I have the opportunity to wander around if I need to."

At that moment Holly walked in, ready for her shift.

"Oh, there she is," Smidgeon said. "Holly, can I have a quick word?"

"Sure."

"Let's go outside," Smidgeon said and she led the way out and around the side of the building. "There ain't much privacy in there."

"What's this about? Is there news about Dave?"

"No, nothing there yet. Mule and Lance are heading up into New Mexico tomorrow. It's about you."

"Mule found out about me." Holly lowered her eyes. "That's it, isn't it?"

"Why don't you tell me yourself?"

"I admit I've had my share of some trouble in the past. Stealing. It was wrong. I know it now. I spent six months in prison for it. It was stupid, kid stuff. You get away with it once and then you think it's no big deal and you do it again. Then you think, maybe just a little more and you convince yourself you'll pay it back, but you never do. That was the longest six months of my life, and I spent every single minute thinking long and hard about what I'd done. I paid back what I could to make amends and resolved I was never going back to that place again if I could help it." Tears were streaming down her face and she trembled as she completed her story.

Smidgeon reached around the sobbing woman and hugged her tight. "It must feel really good to let all of that out."

Holly sniffed and rubbed her nose with the back of her hand. "It does."

"Now, what about your name? He said it wasn't Slidell, it's Shankston."

"That Mule is quite an investigator, isn't he? But he missed something, though. Slidell is my maiden name. The other side of the story is that I was married to a lowlife named Bruce Shankston for less than a year. When I was arrested, I had that name. In truth, he actually encouraged me to steal. He was shacked up with some floozy when I got out, and that's when I divorced him and took my old name back. You can look it all up if you want."

"That's okay, I believe you." Smidgeon moved a stray hair out of Holly's face. "Now, let's go freshen you up and get to work before the rush starts, okay?"

"So I still have a job?"

"Of course you do. I just wanted you to tell me about it. I guess I can't blame you...I never really had you fill out an application or anything."

"What about the extra hours when Lance leaves?"

"Yeah, that hasn't changed, but that means more money for you, right? It also means a lot more work. Lance does a lot all over the place...I'll have to fill in, so that means you'll be pretty much working all the tables."

"Doesn't matter, you've been splitting your tips with me anyway."

"Just till you get on your feet." Smidgeon giggled.

They returned to the dining room and Holly rushed into the restroom.

Smidgeon told Sam, "She spilled all the beans. Slidell is her maiden name. Shankston is her married name; she got divorced."

"Well, that explains most of it."

"She said six months of prison cured her of any desire to return to a life of crime."

"Still, her missing boyfriend is an ex-con."

"And he isn't involved in a crime here either, as far as we know. Treasure hunting could be seen as a way of trying to get ahead without crime and, as you well know, anybody can get obsessed with the thought of treasure."

He smiled. "Point taken."

Four ranch hands removed their hats and sat at a table.

"Guess the lunch rush is starting," Smidgeon said, turning toward the table where she gave them all menus. "Holly will be right with you gentlemen."

"Hey, lady, we ain't no gentlemen, we work for a living," one of them joked.

When Holly emerged, Sam noted that her makeup had been restored and she seemed ready to work. After she took the four orders, she passed by the register, placed her hand on the counter and leaned in close to whisper, "I saw you watching. You don't have to worry about me, Sam."

"Hey, I just work here. Sorry if you thought I was watching you. What else am I supposed to do sitting here on my duff all day?"

She turned to the kitchen, giving him a sidelong glance as she walked away.

Sam returned to his copy of the *El Paso Times* and tried to ignore the thought that something was still not quite right about Holly. He couldn't put his finger on it, but he still had an uncomfortable feeling about her.

"Perhaps Loot was right," he mused quietly to himself. "We'll have to wait and see."

Five

"I figure this trip will only take a couple of days, well, unless something turns up," Mule said as he was loading a beat-up duffle bag into the trunk of his 1983 Oldsmobile Cutlass Supreme.

"You've been living in my house for several months, but this is the first time you've let me ride in your Olds. You usually make me take my truck."

Mule smirked. "I don't trust that truck on a long trip like this. That rust bucket is okay if I think I'm close enough to walk home. Besides, this lady is a gas guzzler. I'd rather ride around in town with you paying for the gas."

Lance loaded his bag and closed the trunk. "At least it's not too far."

"I figure it will take at least five hours. That will give us some time to poke around and find a place to stay. We can really do some digging tomorrow. After that, we'll see." Mule was already buckled into the driver's seat.

Lance leaned into the open passenger door. "Let's see, bags packed and loaded, Prewash is over at Sam and Smidgeon's, the door's locked. I guess I'm ready. Are you ready?"

"Get in the car, Lance."

Once they were underway, as they were passing the small ranges of mountains north of Van Horn, Lance commented, "Haven't been up this way in a while."

"Best way I know to head to the north is to drive north. This is near where y'all found that gold mine you're always yammering about, isn't it?"

"Yep, off that way," Lance said, pointing to the left.

"Ever find anything?"

"Naw. And the rancher has pretty near bankrupted himself looking with heavy equipment."

"Wish I'da known you guys back then. Would have given you some solid advice."

"You know about gold mining?"

"No, I don't. And neither did you. That would have been the main part of my advice."

"I wish it was that easy." Lance fumbled with his sunglasses.

"I know. Look at the stuff we're messing with now. It's involving the same gol'darned foolishness."

"Probably."

Mule glared at Lance. "What do you mean, probably?"

"I got me a funny feeling about Holly."

"I have to admit, I do, too. Something doesn't quite add up." Mule braked slightly as a roadrunner darted across the road.

They made good time as they crossed the New Mexico state line and continued north. They stopped for lunch in Roswell at a small café on the main highway.

39

Mule parked and turned to Lance. "Miss Smidgeon told me this is where Holly used to work. Might be a good place to start asking questions."

Lance said, "And get some food, I hope. My stomach is gnawing on my backbone."

When they had finished eating, the waitress wandered by with more coffee. "Top off your cups?"

"Much obliged. Say, have you worked here long?"

"A year or so, why?"

"We've been wondering about an old buddy of ours who we heard was hanging around Roswell. David Adams. Ever heard of him?"

She scowled. "Oh, Holly's boyfriend. I honestly don't know what she saw in that loser."

"Holly?" Lance asked. "Is she here?"

"No, she cleared out several weeks ago. I miss that girl, she was all right. But that Dave...ugh. He was a low life."

"Sorry to hear that."

"Listen, mister, I'd just forget that guy. I don't know what kind of buddy he was to you, but if I was you, I'd just forget about him, even if he owed me money."

"Well, thanks for the coffee."

"Of course," she said with a smile.

After they finished their coffee and paid, they were almost to Mule's car when a man approached them. "Excuse me. I couldn't help overhearing, you were asking about Dave Adams?"

"Maybe," Mule said.

"What you want with him?" The guy's eyes darted between Mule and Lance.

Mule stared at the man. "I'd say that is our business."

"Maybe it's my business, too. Do you know where he is?"

"How should I know?" Mule answered. "Would I be asking about him if I knew where he was?"

Lance interjected, "We all seem to be just going around in circles here."

The guy turned to Lance and put both hands on hips. "What's it to you, bozo?" He stared for a couple of seconds before reaching into his pocket.

Mule already had a hand ready to grab for his shoulder holster when the guy pulled out a badge.

"Detective Fred Michaels, Roswell PD. I'm sorry, I should have led with that. Now, what do you want with Dave Adams?"

Mule put both palms forward. "Hold on. I'm a private investigator. Can I show you my identification?"

"Sure, but move nice and slow."

Mule pulled out his driver's license and PI credentials.

"Texas, huh? I guess you know you're not licensed to practice in New Mexico."

"I understand that. I'm just making a few informal inquiries for a friend."

"Would your friend be Holly Slidell?"

"Well, she's a friend of a friend."

He turned to Lance. "And who are you?"

"Lance Norton. Friend of the same friend. Just a citizen riding along."

After checking Lance's identification, the detective loosened up a bit. "Okay, sorry for the tough cop bit. My ears just perked up when I heard the name. He's been missing for a while and even stranger, his empty truck turned up over in Lincoln County."

"I've got a friend with the state police and he told me the same thing. You guys have any other interest in this guy?"

"Possible violation of parole, but even that isn't set in stone as of yet. Just hearsay. State boys and Lincoln County asked us about him. We heard he had been consorting with some other paroled felons, but we have no proof. What do you know?"

"He might have been treasure hunting, at least that's what we were told. That's why I brought Lance here. He has some experience in that sort of thing."

Detective Michaels' eyes brightened. "Wait, Lance Norton? I thought that name sounded familiar. You were involved in that Sublett Mine incident—the serial killer down there. Oh, and that guy running a crime syndicate out of Mexico. Both things were all over the news. That was you?"

Lance sighed and looked away. "My fame has preceded me."

Mule interjected, "So, any idea what became of the truck?"

"It was towed from Arabela where it was found. I think it's probably in Capitan at a car shop there. Usually these things go to the closest place. State boys went over it pretty good but found nothing."

"Can you point us in that direction? Arabela, I mean. I want to take a look around the spot where the truck was abandoned."

"Just be careful poking around. Remember, your investigator license is no good here."

Mule laughed. "I did this even before I got officially licensed, so I pretty much know what I can do and what I can't do."

Michaels handed Mule a card. "Well, if you do happen to find him, could you give me a heads up?"

"Yes I will. You've been a big help."

After receiving some directions to Arabela, Mule and Lance were on their way.

"Nice guy," Lance said, adding, "sort of."

"Just doing his job." Mule chuckled. "You handle yourself with investigative work pretty well. You're quiet when you need to be, and then you give a measured response where it is most useful. We were rapidly getting on each other's nerves and you diffused the situation."

"Look, buddy, I ain't looking to get arrested or killed in New Mexico. So what do you expect to find in this Arabela place?"

"Not a darned thing."

~ * ~

"The lunch rush is over, Holly, why don't' you take a load off and get a bite to eat? What can I get you?"

"I want to try one of those Best Danged Burgers. I've served a bunch of them, so I'm intrigued."

"Good idea. I haven't had one in a while myself, so I think I'll join you." On her way to the kitchen, Smidgeon called back, "Sam! You want a BDB?"

Sam was reading the paper over by the register with his injured leg propped up. "Sure, sounds good."

He grabbed his crutches and made his way over to Holly's table. "Mind if I join you?"

"Of course."

"You seem to be settling in," Sam said.

"I don't know about that. Waitressing is mostly knowing the subtleties of the menu, and I still have a way to go with that. Most of the customers are regulars, so it's been easier since they already know what they want."

Sam fiddled with the condiments. "Yep, they'll keep you on track. They know some of our routines better than we do. I went through the same thing."

"So you haven't worked here long?"

"A couple of years."

"And you ended up with the boss."

"We were together before I started working here. I was a customer when we met, just passing through. I lived in Austin back then."

"Wow, that's pretty far. I hear Austin is wonderful. Why'd you decide to move to a backwater like this?"

"It's not that bad," he said. "I like the pace."

"Well, I'm happy to be working with such nice folks. Listen, Sam, you know, if you ever want to..."

Smidgeon bounded through the swinging door with three steaming plates.

"Get them while they're hot," she said. "And before we get any customers."

Holly admired the sandwich. "So, what's the Best Danged Burger all about?"

Sam said, "Lance came up with this. I mean, how can you go wrong? Guacamole, bacon, pimento cheese..."

"I love our pimento cheese!"

Smidgeon beamed, "It's my mama's recipe. It's the best."

Holly took a huge bite and almost dropped food out of her grinning mouth. "It is, it really is the best danged burger I've ever tasted!"

"Hence, the name," Sam said, handing her a napkin. "But it's a bit messy."

After Holly finished her burger, she continued munching on fries and said, "Glad it slacked off for a while. This place gets really busy."

"Yeah, wish I could spell you," Sam said.

"Oh, it's nothing I can't handle. I just need to get back into the swing of things. Have you heard from Lance or Mule yet?"

Sam said, "They're probably only getting there about now. Mule is very methodical so he'll take his time."

Holly's eyes teared. "I told myself I wasn't going to cry."

Smidgeon reached out and held Holly's hand. "Just don't worry. The boys will turn up something."

Holly squeezed Smidgeon's hand but her eyes turned to Sam and she winked.

~ * ~

"So this is Arabela," Lance said with a sigh. "Ain't much to look at."

"Just a conglomeration of residences like most small places out in the middle of nowhere," Mule added. He stopped his car and approached a man working on the outside of his house. After a short conversation, he returned.

"He said the truck was found down the side road a few hundred yards from here. He also said he works at the ranch down that same road and the owners aren't there right now. He's going to get his trail bike and lead us to the spot.

They heard the whine of a two-cycle motorcycle engine and a helmeted figure waved at them as he came racing around the side of the house. They followed as he headed down the paved road, then slowed and turned down an unpaved road. They proceeded a mile or so and the man braked and got off his bike. Mule and Lance got out of the car.

"This way, not far," the man said, extending a hand to Lance. "Mark Lucas," he said.

"Lance."

They walked about two hundred feet up what looked like a worn jeep trail. There was an oil stain in the parched landscape. "That's the spot."

Lance squatted and rubbed the stain, then smelled his fingers. "Oil's thick and pretty fresh. They didn't think he broke down, but I'd say there's a good bet he bottomed out on one of those deep ruts we walked over and dinged his oil pan."

"That's what I told them." Mark continued, "But them state police boys said they knew better."

"Any idea where they would have taken it?" Mule asked.

"We don't get a lot of abandoned vehicles around here, but I recognized the name on the tow truck. It was from Capitan."

"How far is it?"

"Less than forty miles, but it will be getting late by the time you get there. There's a nice motel, though, and a couple of places to eat.'

"Appreciate it."

Mule walked in a wide circle. "Is there a trail toward the wilderness area?"

"Mister, there's trails all over out here, but they is tricky. Sometimes they're wildlife trails, sometimes they're dry stream beds, and sometimes they're ragged jeep trails like this. Most fools I've seen venturing out into the wilderness area are looking for Archangel."

"I've thought that maybe it's what our boy was doing," Mule said. "What do you know about Archangel?"

"I think it's a bunch of hooey. But if you're going to Capitan, there's a guy there, Mitch Blalock, who knows a lot about it. He's sort of a local expert on the myth."

"How do we find him?"

"Just ask. Everybody knows him. He's a bit of a town character."

They hiked back down to the vehicles.

"Mister, you'd do better to drive on down to the ranch house and turn around. It will be much easier for you than backing out. Just be careful for those deep ruts. I figured that guy probably tried it in when it was getting on toward dark and couldn't see what he was doing."

"Many thanks, Mark," Lance said.

Back at the crossroads, Mule studied his map. "Guess we're heading to Capitan," he said.

Six

"Nice to have you working in the back again," Chuy the cook told Smidgeon as she labored over a pile of dishes in the sink.

"It's running me ragged though," she said.

"Manny will be here later; he'll wash the plates."

"There's no time. We have to keep on top of them or we'll run out," she said.

Holly came in with another order and Smidgeon dried her hands after loading the drying rack and prepared to expedite the order. For her, this was a never ending cycle. She glanced out the small window to the dining room.

"Again?" she whispered to herself as she saw Holly chatting with Sam at the register. "Seems to me every time I look out she's over there," she said under her breath.

She saw Chuy pushing another two plates under the heat lamp.

"Don't hit the bell, I see them." She added, "I'm sick of that darned bell."

Smidgeon navigated the doors with a plate in each hand and delivered the order. The moment she emerged, Holly turned abruptly from the register area and returned to her duties. Smidgeon scowled at Sam who returned a questioning look before shrugging.

He's a smart boy; he knows I'm ticked off.

After the breakfast rush was over, Smidgeon saw Holly go out the front door, probably to have a cigarette, so she approached Sam. "Is she bothering you?"

Sam sighed. "I know, she keeps coming over here. Flirty, too. But you don't have anything to worry about."

"Oh, I know that. You're the one who needs to do any worrying. Just don't encourage her."

"I haven't been. But I'm bored stiff out here. I'm not used to being so immobile."

"I know, and I'm sorry. It is what it is."

"Want me to say something?" Sam asked.

"Just don't encourage her. I'm not the jealous type, but...well, there's something about her. She reminds me of the girls in school we used to call boy crazy."

Sam chuckled. "I kind of like two women fighting over me."

"Listen, you..."

"But seriously, I haven't been giving her any encouragement. It's been mostly small talk, but then again..."

"What?"

"It's small talk that always seems to get flirtier the longer it goes on. I'll try to keep a lid on it."

"You know, you can tell her to get back to work. Technically this is my café, but Lordy, Sam, you're number two here. You can certainly act with authority. I give you permission."

Sam smiled. "Ah, so it's a power kinda deal. I like power."

"Just keep your pants zipped, *el jefe*."

~ * ~

"Pretty typical small mountain town," Mule observed.

"Billy the Kid country," Lance said.

"That's right, there was a lot of trouble here at one time. They called it the Lincoln County War…"

"I noticed something else. Everything is called Smoky Bear this or that."

"If I remember the story correctly, they found a cub near here after a big forest fire and made him the mascot and hero of fire prevention. We know him now as Smoky Bear."

"No kidding?"

"It's the gospel truth," Mule said.

Lance pointed at a motel. "Well, let's check out the Smoky Bear Motel and Restaurant. Maybe we can ask about that Blalock guy."

After they secured a room, they went into the adjacent restaurant.

Lance gave the menu a thorough examination. "It's always interesting to check out other operations."

"You haven't always worked in restaurants, have you?"

"Naw. For the last several years I mostly did ranch work, but I worked at several food joints in high school and college. It's funny, I always hated those jobs back then. It was just the means to an end, but being part of Smidgeon's crew has been way different."

"Has a lot to do with the people."

"That's very true. We all get along and, well, it just feels good to be a part of Smidgeon's place. Sam and Smidgeon are just about the best friends I've had as an adult."

49

Mule looked over the top of his reading glasses at Lance.

"Oh, and you, too, of course," Lance added.

Mule resumed reading his menu. "Thanks."

As the waitress topped off their coffee, she asked, "Will that be all?"

Lance said, "Yeah, and it was all great. Thank you."

"Say," Mule interjected. "I was wondering about an old buddy of mine, Mitch Blaylock. Is he still around?"

"Oh, Mitch? Sure. You head back out this way and turn down Billy-the-Kid Trail. His place has a sign that says "Curios" out front. The place looks a little ratty, just like him, I guess."

Mule chuckled. "Sounds like Mitch."

They paid, followed the directions, and stopped at a run-down building with a faded sign pronouncing "BLALOCK'S CURIOS" but the first word was almost completely faded so the second word seemed to stand out.

They walked up to the door and Lance said, "Doesn't look open."

"No, it doesn't," Mule added, after he rattled the door knob. "But that's not surprising. It's late."

After they turned toward the car, they heard a deadbolt click.

"What you want?"

Mule spun around. "Mitch Blalock?"

"Yeah, who are you?"

"Name's Mule Hollis. I'm a private investigator."

"I don't know nothing."

"It's not like that. I'm tracking a guy who disappeared—we think he was looking for Archangel."

Blalock took a step forward and furtively glanced left and right. "Then he's more than likely looking for trouble. Come on in. If you were asking about it anyplace else, they musta sent you to me."

He locked the door behind them, and they made their way past shelves and tables of dusty artifacts.

"Sorry for the clutter. Getting too old and tired to mess much with the store these days. You two just keep heading back. I live here. I gots me an apartment back there." He pointed past the big room to a curtain where a light was showing.

They emerged into a tidy efficiency apartment with a TV blaring next to one wall. On the opposite wall there was a small couch.

"That's a fold-out. Sleeps mighty comfy, too. You boys want some coffee? I was just heating some water when you rattled at my door."

"Sure," Lance said.

Blalock busied himself in the kitchenette, tapping a spoon each time as he emptied the instant coffee crystals into three mugs, then he poured steaming water. "Sugar?"

"Yeah, just a touch," Mule said. The distinctive aroma of instant coffee filled the room.

"Got cubes."

"One, then."

"I'll take one," Lance said.

When he delivered the coffee, he settled in. His hair was mussed and he had two or three days' of mottled gray and brown bits of beard on his face, but his dark brown eyes were alert and clear.

"So, Archangel, huh?"

"That's what we think he was looking for."

"Been a couple of people asking about it in the last month. Unusual because it's off-season. Ever few years, the story gets resurrected and a few hardy souls will attempt to find it, no matter the season."

"What is Archangel, exactly?"

"That's part of the mystery. Nobody really knows."

"I like a good mystery. Tell us more," Lance said.

"Well, many people expand it and call it, the Archangel Cache, but it is more correctly termed The Saint Michael the Archangel Cache."

"That's a mouthful," Mule said, pretending he hadn't heard this before.

"Exactly, which is why everyone shortens it. As the story goes, in 1773 an expedition was heading south toward Mexico with a shipment of gold and silver from the mines near the missions of Santa Fe. They were ambushed by a band of either bandits or maybe even Apaches; no one knows for sure. But whoever it was, they laid siege to the small group. They eventually retreated toward the Capitan Mountains, where they found an outcropping of rocks that provided at least some protection. As the story goes, they thought the treasure was only slowing them down, so they buried the riches they were carrying and attempted to escape."

Mule emptied his cup. "Makes sense, if it was a lot of gold. How much we talking about?"

"Again, no one knows for sure, but legends like this don't persist unless it was a lot. Anyway, they were low on supplies and thought if they could break through to some form of safety, they might be able to return later and reclaim the buried cache."

"Seems a good plan," Mule interjected, "but their assailants obviously had a different idea."

"You're right. Only one man from the expedition survived, a soldier named Diego. As the attack continued on the dwindling caravan, he was knocked from his horse and hit his head. Before he lost consciousness, he remembered the group's leader, Padre de la Garza, giving him the last rites of the church before falling himself. Diego woke up during a thunderstorm and realized he was the only one alive. The remains of the party had been plundered, but he found an upturned bowl that had been left. It was full of rainwater. He drank from it and collected enough water in the downpour to fill it twice more. After that he somehow managed to find his way to a hacienda many miles away."

Lance leaned forward, "And the cache?"

"He had been disoriented by the ordeal. He knew they fled toward the east from *Camino Real de Tierra Adentro*. Over many years he made several attempts to find the cache, but all failed."

"And why was it called the Archangel Cache?" Mule asked.

"Diego said they buried it on the feast day honoring Saint Michael the Archangel. September twenty-ninth. Padre de la Garza took that as a sign from heaven that the cache would be protected by St. Michael until one of them returned to retrieve it."

"But no one ever did," Lance said.

"Like I said, Diego searched his entire life and died broke and disheartened."

"That's a miserable way to go through life," Lance said.

Mule added, "You got that right. So nobody ever found it?"

"One theory is that Apaches found it, dug it up and the treasure was dispersed to the four winds. There are Mescalero legends that speak of such things, returning the purloined precious metals to the earth."

"Bull," Mule said. "By then, even Apaches knew the value of gold and silver."

"Exactly what I've always thought," Mitch said. "Most people think it is still out there. Truth is, nobody knows."

"Aren't there any other clues?"

"Theories, but not clues. Diego was stunned by his fall. He knew the area was surrounded by rocks, but he didn't remember much more. He thought it was close to Capitan Peak because when they fled east, they lost their way. They were seeking refuge to defend against the attacks. So, most searchers have concentrated between the Capitan and Sunset peaks. It's rough country."

"So you said a couple of people had asked you about it recently?"

"Yeah, the first guy seemed pretty standard," Mitch scratched his chin. "Let's see, I think he said his name was Dave."

Lance and Mule exchanged glances, then Lance said, "That's the name of the guy we're interested in."

"Young fella, sandy hair. Didn't seem to have even a clue of what he was doing, though. Remember his beat-up Dodge truck. Didn't see any hiking equipment in the back either."

Mule asked, "You said there was another one, too."

"Some people just give off a feeling of bad news, and this guy was like that. I could feel the hair on the back of my neck standing on end while I was talking to him."

"And why did Dave and this other guy look you up?"

"Same as you fellas, I guess. I know as much about the Archangel Cache as anybody, but that reputation is a bit off the mark."

"How's that?" Lance asked.

"I know the history of it. Its location is so vague and obscure, there is no way to know more than that. It's a frustrating reality to most people who contact me. I can only tell them what I know. I can't tell them what I don't know."

"You mean where the treasure is." Lance chuckled. "If you knew much of anything, you'd already have found the treasure for yourself and they wouldn't need to be asking."

"I'd have a lot nicer a store, I tell you that! But it's still good for business."

"How's that?" Mule asked.

"Every time the story gets a boost, so does the tourist money around here."

"Makes sense," Lance said.

Mule got back to business, "Well, this Dave fellow's truck was found over near Arabela and brought here."

"I heard about a truck being found. That was his?"

"We assume so. We want to take a look at it if we can find it."

"Fella named Joe Bob has a tow service. He's probably the one the police called. He's on the edge of town." Mitch looked toward a small window behind him. "Getting onto dark now, you'll have to check in the morning."

"We'll do it," Mule said, heading back through the shelves toward the front of the building.

Mitch unlocked the door and said, "One other thing."

They both turned around and Lance said, "What's that?"

"There was another guy in the car with that last guy. And they didn't ask about the Archangel so much as they asked about anybody else asking, which I took to mean that Dave fella."

"Not your typical treasure hunters?"

"Not at all. That's probably why I found them so odd. I didn't tell them he'd been here, just a little about what most people are usually looking for. I'd just be careful of them if you cross their path."

"What kind of car did they drive?" Mule asked.

"It was early evening, so I can't tell you what make it was, but it was a big black thing."

"Big black vehicle. Okay. That's not much to go on, but we'll be careful."

~ * ~

Holly was scrubbing the coffee station counter. "I can help Sam close tonight if you want to take the evening off. I don't mind at all."

Smidgeon was filling salt shakers at the nearest table. She smiled at Holly. "I appreciate the offer, but I think Sam and I can handle it okay. Besides, I'm his ride."

Holly disappeared into the kitchen and Smidgeon muttered under her breath, "Yeah, you can close with Sam when pigs can fly."

"What, honey?" Sam had maneuvered behind her on his crutches.

"Nothing," she said.

"I heard you. Really, I think she's just got a flirty streak, you know, it's her personality. Lots of waitresses do. It's good for tips. You used to flirt with me, too."

"Yeah, and look what happened."

He sat down. "I guess you may have something there. So it's out of my control, right?"

"You'll stop right there, buster, unless you want me to kick your leg. Now fill those pepper shakers." She got up and began to distribute the salt shakers around the tables.

"Yes, ma'am."

Holly returned from the kitchen and sat next to Sam, "Oh, Sam, let me do that!"

Smidgeon tried not to react but she noted Holly looking at her while she reached across Sam.

"No, really, I've got this. Why don't you go ahead and clock out. Manny can fix you something to take with you."

"But you are supposed to take it easy," Holly said.

"Right...take it easy on my *leg*. My hands and fingers are just fine."

She looked across the room at Smidgeon. "Is that what you want?"

"We've got it, you go on and get yourself something to eat and head out, okay?"

"Fine," she said as she turned abruptly and disappeared into the kitchen.

Smidgeon grabbed a handful of pepper shakers. "See what I mean?"

"I'll try to let her down easy."

When Holly came out with a small sack, she said, "I wish Mule or Lance would call. I'd really like to know if they've found anything."

"Well, they've barely had time to look," Sam said.

~ * ~

"Seventy-five Dodge?" a guy with the name Joe Bob embroidered on his shirt rubbed a grease smudge onto his jawline, "Yeah, the state boys called me to pick one up a few days ago, way off in Arabela. Abandoned down a dead end, unpaved road."

"Nobody's called for it?"

"No, the po-lice are checking the registration and will give me their report paperwork. I'll store it a while waiting on the owner, then there's a process for me to take it as salvage if nobody claims it and pays the towing and storage. That mounts up in a hurry, so most people never claim them."

Mule showed his PI license. "I'm an investigator looking for the owner of that truck. Any chance I could give it a once over?"

"Now, mister, I don't pretend to know a whole lot in this world, but I know one thing for sure. If you show me a Texas license, you ain't no PI in New Mexico."

"I understand that, but..."

"Shucks, mister, I don't give a dolly ding dang, I's just funning you. Sure you can take a look. State boys already took their own look, though. Warn't much to find."

"Yeah, but I'm an ex-cop, so I'd still like to give it a try."

Joe Bob led them through the storage yard to a rusty white pickup. "She ain't much to look at, but I don't see she's in such bad shape."

"Did you start her?" Lance asked.

"Nope, no call for that. I think the cops did, though."

Lance got on his back and inched his way underneath the engine, then squirmed back out and stood. "Just as I thought. Nick in the oil pan." He opened the hood and pulled the dip stick. "Dry."

"Well, I'll be," Joe Bob exclaimed.

"Lance, I wondered about your theory, but looks like you're right."

"Darned tooting I'm right."

"How did you know that?" Joe Bob repeated the dip stick test. "Dry as a bone."

"Guy in Arabela showed us where the truck had been sitting. It was pretty obvious it had lost a lot of oil."

"Heck of a place for a breakdown. Why was he down that dead end road?"

"That's what we're trying to figure out," Mule said. He peered into the open door, then went around and examined the passenger side, even emptying the contents of the glove compartment. He flipped the lever and allowed the passenger seat to swing forward.

"What's this?" he said.

Joe Bob and Lance huddled close behind to see where Mule was pointing.

Lance said, "There's a danged tear in the upholstery seam!"

Mule chuckled, "It's an old trick. They cut the stitching right along the seam then sticky it up with something to hold it together." He gently spread the open seam, thrust his hand into the void and pulled out an army-style .45 automatic. He removed the clip and examined it. "Fully loaded." He reached in again and retrieved two small boxes. "More ammo."

"I guess whatever happened, he didn't have time to grab his gun," Lance said. "Wonder why he had it hidden like that?"

"Convicted felon," Mule said. "It's something I've seen before with this sort of guy. Possession of a handgun is a parole violation. That's one of the reasons I wanted to see the truck."

"So we know he's unarmed."

"*Probably* unarmed. This could have been his backup piece, considering the fact it was on the passenger side."

Mule thrust his hand into the space one more time and, after feeling around, he extracted a folded up piece of paper and handed it to Lance.

Lance unfolded the sheet and read it. "Looks like some kind of directions. If he didn't take it along, he must not be heading to where it leads. Or he's trying to do it from memory." He handed it to Mule.

"Starts in Arabela, though. I guess we're going back."

"What about the gun?" Joe Bob asked.

"Call the state police and tell them you noticed the rip and found it along with the ammo."

Job Bob asked, "And the note?"

Mule handed Joe Bob a twenty dollar bill, "Maybe we can just keep that between us."

Joe Bob opened his mouth in a wide smile that showed most of his remaining teeth. "Okay, mister."

On the way back to the motel, Lance asked, "So what's our next move?"

"You're the trainee detective, what do you think our next move should be?"

"We're only five hours or so from home, I say we go back and show this note to Sam and Smidgeon. They've both got a lot more experience with this sort of thing."

"What about Dave?" Mule asked.

"They were able to start the truck without ruining the engine, so I don't think he knew about the oil leak. I still think he parked his truck and got out of it for some reason before he was snatched. I figure he might have been heading up that trail to get away from somebody. Our next step would be to follow where this note leads, but we can't go traipsing off without equipment. Sam probably has most of what we need." Lance glanced over the note again. "And if anybody can make more sense out of these scribblings, my money would be on Sam."

"Well, let's go check out of the motel and get on the road."

Seven

Sam shifted on his stool as he sat behind the register, trying to accommodate the persistent aching in his leg.

Holly noticed his discomfort. "You okay, Sam?"

"My leg's just hurting a little today," he said, pointing down. "I'm trying to ignore it, but it's taking a while to ease off."

"Did the doctor give you anything for pain?"

"Yeah, but those pills fog up my brain too much."

"Yeah, that's what they do. Say, Sam..." she said, approaching the counter, "since Smidgeon's at the bank, there's something I've been meaning to ask you. It seems like she's always watching me whenever I try to talk to you."

Sam was already wary. "Okay..."

"Do you, I mean, do you and Smidgeon have any kind of...arrangement?"

"I'm not sure what you mean," Sam said, but he knew exactly what she meant.

"Well, I was thinking that if maybe you were interested, maybe I could help take your mind off your leg for a little while. We work together all day and I feel like we, well, uh, we really have a sort of connection. With Dave gone, I've been really lonely, you know?"

"Well, it's not really an arrangement, but I think my options along those lines involve being gutted, stuffed, and then killed. And anyway, wouldn't Dave be bothered by something like that?"

"It's not like we're married or anything, and, by the way, neither are you. Like I said, I'm just lonely, you know?"

"Look, Holly, I like you and all, but you need to understand, I *love* Smidgeon."

"Don't you think I'm attractive?"

"Yes, you're attractive, but you need to get it through your head that I don't want to cheat on Smidgeon. Listen, we've both been trying to *help* you."

She feigned a pout and quickly walked toward the kitchen. "Okay, then...your loss."

Sam tried to read his book, but his head was pounding and his leg was throbbing. He heard Smidgeon's car in the parking lot, so he took a deep breath because he knew he had to tell her about this.

"Hi, sweetie. Wow, it's dead today."

"Yeah, it's been a quiet day."

"What's up?"

"Come around here...we need to talk." Sam stood and grabbed his crutches. When Smidgeon approached, he reached out and gave her a hug.

"Aw," she said. She nuzzled his neck for a few seconds, then pulled her head back and asked, "What's wrong?"

"Nothing major, but Holly just made a pass at me."

Smidgeon took a half-step back. "What?"

"Yeah, big time."

"What did she say?"

"She asked if we had an arrangement."

"What did you say?"

"I told her we didn't and that I wasn't interested. She turned away in a huff and disappeared into the kitchen."

Smidgeon took a deep breath. "Okay. And after all I've done for her...after all *we've* done for her. My Lord, Lance and Mule drove hundreds of miles to try to look for *her* boyfriend. I gave her a job, I paid for a motel room, and *this* is how she repays me?"

"I guess she's just lonely and I'm here. My being pretty much immobile probably doesn't help. And besides," he pointed at himself with both index fingers and said, "Aaaaay," imitating TV's Fonzi as he switched to a thumbs up.

"You idiot. Okay, I'll ignore it for now. You know I was afraid of something like this, but it sounds like you handled it okay."

"Well, I haven't been totally honest. My first response was that my understanding of our arrangement was that if I didn't behave, I'd be gutted, stuffed, then killed."

"Ah, so you *do* understand our arrangement." Smidgeon raised one eyebrow.

"Deeply," he said and he reached out and drew her back to him for a kiss.

"I'm not sure I deserve you. Just keep being good."

"Always," Sam said.

~ * ~

Mule and Lance drove into the parking lot just as Smidgeon was preparing to lock the door for the night. She opened the door and greeted them as they came in. "Good timing, I was just locking up when I saw you drive up. Didn't expect you so soon."

"Well, we didn't go too far, not really," Lance said. "And there was not much else we could do without touching base here."

Mule brought up the rear. "Howdy, Miss Smidgeon. Any chance we could get a bite?"

"Everything's shut down but the oven is probably still hot, so I can maybe heat up a plate or two of today's special, *Texicali Arroz con Pollo*. I think we had a little left over."

"Sounds great," Lance said.

Sam called out, "I'm just finishing the register. Sit down and I'll be over in a minute."

"Take your time. I'll get us some drinks," Lance said.

Mule settled into a chair while Lance retrieved a couple of Cokes.

Sam soon joined them and asked, "What did you find out?"

"Not much," Mule said.

Lance responded, "Well, we did come across a couple of interesting things. Is Holly here? She'll probably want to hear what we dug up."

"No, she went on to the motel. Smidgeon will be out in a minute. I think we should at least wait for her."

She poked her head into the dining room from the kitchen. "I heard that. You bet you're going to wait for me. In fact, while you eat, I think I'll go fetch Holly."

"Good idea," Lance said.

In a few minutes, Smidgeon came out with three steaming plates on a tray. "Ain't nothing fancy."

Sam looked up. "Oh, one for me, too?"

"I'm pretty sure I won't have time to fix anything at the house."

"What about you?"

"I'm fine. I'll grab a sandwich or something. Okay, I'm heading to the motel."

Dolings Motel was just a short drive and as she pulled into the back parking lot, Smidgeon saw Holly's car outside an open door. She parked, and as she approached the room, she saw Holly through the window. She was in the process of packing her bags.

"Holly, what are you doing?"

"If you've come here to have it out with me, you don't have to bother."

"Oh, the thing with Sam? He told me all about it."

Holly stopped and stared. "I figured he would. He's a strange one. You're lucky. I guess he's one of the rare good men in the world. I'm sorry, Smidgeon, I don't know what came over me."

"Some gals just can't get past the notion of not having a man in their life. Took me a few trips through those revolving doors before I figured out it doesn't have to be that way."

"I guess you're right."

"Look, at first I was really mad, but after talking things over with Sam, I'm willing to give you the benefit of the doubt. But that isn't why I came by."

"It isn't?"

"No. Mule and Lance are back. I thought we should all be there together to hear what they have to say. Now if you're dead set on leaving, I can't stop you, but they went to a lot of trouble to help you and I think you owe them some consideration."

"You're right." She dropped the blouse she was holding back in the drawer. "Let's go."

Holly grabbed her key and followed Smidgeon outside. "Come on with me. I'll bring you back."

Holly lowered her head. "You sure?"

Smidgeon turned to face her. "Listen, I don't like what you did. Not one little bit. Oh, I understand the woman part, but the people part? Going after Sam behind my back? It's a mystery to me. But overall, I like you, Holly. You helped me when I needed help, and when you came here with some troubles, we have all tried to band together to help you. Just settle in, and we'll see if we can keep you safe while we find out what the heck is going on. Okay?"

Holly nodded and got into the car.

At the café, Lance was gathering up the empty plates when Smidgeon walked in. "Oh, man, what a lucky day to get back. That is my favorite special. It really hit the spot."

"I sure like it," Mule said.

"Just leftovers," Smidgeon said, "But happy to oblige."

Holly came in behind Smidgeon, "Hey, everybody."

Mule stood and nodded to her. "Miss Holly. Pull up another chair and sit down."

When the five were seated, Mule started talking. "When we got to Roswell, we happened to meet a detective named Michaels."

"Fred Michaels?" Holly asked.

"Yes."

"He's a regular at the place where I used to work."

"That's where we saw him. He heard us mentioning your boyfriend's name. Roswell PD is interested in talking to him, too."

"What for?"

"Possible parole violation."

"I should have figured that. He's not supposed to consort with his prison buddies."

Mule tapped his index finger on the table as he continued. "In practice, it isn't usually a big problem. It's almost impossible to enforce unless illegal stuff crops up, and then it's sure an easy way to draw attention to yourself."

"Dave wasn't doing anything illegal."

"Did you know he had a forty-five automatic hidden in his truck?"

Holly's shocked expression preceded a distinct stammer, "No...no, I...I...I didn't."

"That is a big problem for him. His truck, his gun. Definitely illegal for a parolee."

"Damn you, Dave," she muttered.

Lance interrupted. "Mule here found that after the state police missed it."

"Seriously?" Sam said. "I'm impressed."

"I was a cop for years...you learn things. State police stationed in a backwater like that are likely less experienced than a seasoned cop. Don't forget, I worked in a crossroads town right off the Interstate. He used a pretty good technique and did a slick job of it, too. He slit the seam on the back of the upholstery then smoothed it with something sticky. I'm not surprised they missed it."

"What gets me is how criminals," Smidgeon noticed Holly spin her head when she said that word, "Sorry, Holly...how people figure out how to do stuff like that."

"Going to prison is like going to crime trade school," Lance said. "People got nothing but time on their hands, and they share everything they know."

"Exactly right. Also found this." Mule reached into his shirt pocket, retrieved a folded piece of paper, and handed it to Holly. "Ever seen this?"

She read it. "No...It looks like a bunch of gibberish."

Mule retrieved the paper and handed it to Sam. "Maybe you can shed a little more light on it."

Sam read over the paper silently for a minute. "Arabela, that's where the truck was found, right?" Mule nodded and Sam continued reading.

"What do you think?" Lance asked.

"It's definitely rough directions to find something. See here?" he said, pointing to the paper, "'3 1/2 mi wnw Arabela' obviously means one should head, walk probably, three and a half miles in that direction with Arabela as a starting point. It mentions landmarks like a split tree, a rock triangle, and a saddle. It's a jumbled mess to read here, but if somebody was on the ground out there, it all might start to make some sense."

A tear rolled down Holly's face. "So you think Dave is out there trying to follow it?"

Sam said, "I don't know. If it was me, with directions this complicated, I'd sure want it in my hands to look at. Memorizing something like this can get tricky."

"Maybe he made a copy," Smidgeon said.

Sam shook his head. "Maybe, but if you're treasure hunting, you don't want a lot of copies of anything floating around."

"I agree with Sam," Mule retorted. "Plus, I think he would have taken his forty-five. That's why both things were hidden together."

"But why'd he leave his truck?" Holly asked. "They said it wasn't broken down."

"Oh, but it was," Lance answered. "He'd dinged his oil pan. It was a rough road, and he had to know he hit it pretty hard. I've been thinking about that all the way back. I think that at the very least he would have gotten out to take a look, so he probably knew he was losing oil."

"That was another thing the state police missed," Mule added. "Lance here figured that out pretty handily."

"A big oil spot on pristine ground is pretty hard to miss, but when they checked it out, the truck was probably in the way."

Mule continued, "Still, it could explain why he left the truck without taking the gun or the directions. If he got out to look under the truck, somebody could have gotten the drop on him."

"Anyway, I'd say that following these directions probably won't lead us to Dave," Sam said.

"But they might take us where he *wanted* to go. He probably figures Archangel is there," Mule said.

"I'm going to El Paso tomorrow—I was planning to look for more information on the Archangel Cache. I think you should wait until I get back."

"Oh, we found a fella in Capitan who told us all about it," Lance said, and he related the high points of Mitch Blalock's dissertation on the subject.

Sam said, "So, it's probably connected to this trade route. What did he call it?"

"*Camino Real de Tierra Adentro*," Lance said.

"Any idea where Dave got this note?" Sam asked.

"I don't know," Holly said. "But before he left, he seemed pretty sure he could find the treasure."

"That's what it always seems like at first. Well, I can't go off and look for him like this," Sam said, pointing at his leg.

"You're darned tooting you can't," Smidgeon added.

"That's another reason why we came back so soon," Lance said. "I need to borrow some of your hiking kit."

"Sure, you can borrow whatever you need," he said. "And as far as the note is concerned, it seems fairly straightforward, but like I said, you need to be out there to see the landmarks it mentions. Uh..."

"Uh, what?"

"If they're still there. A lot of things can change over the years. You know, stuff like flash floods, forest fires, and hikers picking up or spreading rocks. We have no idea how old this information is. These all look like small local landmarks that could be very fragile. This 'N 500 yards at split tree' could just as well turn out to be north 500 yards from where a split tree *used to be*."

"I didn't think of that."

"And you need to be able to get yourself back. That's the trick in cross-country hiking. Reaching your destination is generally only the halfway point."

Holly asked, "So when can you guys go back?"

"Well, I'm in no shape to hike in those hills…it's pretty rugged," Mule said, "so that will be up to Lance."

"As soon as possible," Lance added.

"Like I said, I'd sure feel better about it if you'd let me finish my El Paso appointment. I could maybe find some helpful maps or other information in the library at UTEP."

"That means two more days," Holly said.

"It's been weeks," Smidgeon said. "And we don't even know if he is out there."

"Yeah, but we have to rule it out. Two more days seems like a long time, but he's already been missing for weeks," Sam said.

"Lance, if you can handle the reins here, I'll drive Sam to El Paso."

"I thought I was going alone this time."

"Yeah, right. Anyway, this will give us two sets of eyes looking for something."

"Well, I'll leave you two to work that out," Lance said, "but sure, I'll handle the café."

Eight

Smidgeon looked up from her chair in the waiting room. Sam limped toward her carrying his crutches in one hand.

She asked, "You're good to walk on your own?"

"Yeah, but I have to take it easy," he said. "That won't be hard, since it's still really sore."

"What good news! But I still want you to stay off your feet at the café. Oh, and don't get any bright ideas about hiking into those mountains."

As they walked to Smidgeon's car, Sam winced a couple of times. "Believe me, I'm pretty sure I'm a long way from doing any hiking."

"There was a student waiting to see the doctor, and she gave me directions to the university library."

"That's a big help. I sure hope we can park close."

"Oh, that's a problem, isn't it?"

"Well, the doc said to use the crutches if I feel I need them, and I think I'll do that as we walk to the library. That way I can save my leg for wandering in the stacks."

At the University of Texas at El Paso, they eventually found a place they could park, and made their way to the library.

Smidgeon said, "I didn't expect it to be so big."

"University libraries always are, but it shouldn't be too hard to find what we need."

Sam started his initial search at the card catalog stacks. He wrote down a few filing locations and said, "Let's go, time for the first pass."

"First pass?"

"Usually, I start by finding a couple of easy references. Similar books will be in the same area, so I'll find the books I wrote down then browse the stacks. If we're lucky, we'll find what we need right away, but we'll probably need to check the bibliographies to find some other suitable works to look up."

"Wow, I had no idea it was so complicated. You really know this stuff."

"I call it returning to student mode. I spent years doing this kind of research."

Sam retrieved a few books and sat at a table to read through them. Smidgeon wandered around the stacks, amazed to glimpse the world she had missed by not attending college out of high school. As she scanned titles at random, a book caught her eye. *Lost Treasure of the Southwest*. She pulled it out and opened it. She had noticed Sam looking in the index, so she tried that, looking for the word Archangel.

There was nothing there, but she flipped a few pages and looked for Saint Michael and there it was, an entry for the Saint Michael the Archangel Cache. She took it over to the table.

"Sam, honey, look what I found."

He seemed perturbed by the interruption when he first glanced up but saw she was holding a book and pointing to something, so he followed her finger and found the magic words.

"How did you find this?"

"I was just poking around."

Sam read through the text. "It's exactly the kind of thing we're looking for."

"I know."

He read with interest, then checked the bibliography and wrote down another title.

"So I did good?" she asked.

"You did great. Now I need to look up another book. Do you think you could go down to the card catalog again for me? Just look up the title and write down the number that looks like this." He showed her his written entries and handed her the paper.

"I'll give it a try."

She found the entry and returned upstairs, but she decided to go Sam one better. She'd seen him finding books based on that number, so she decided she would try to find the book for him. To her delight, she spotted it with no problem and took the book to Sam.

"Here it is. I decided to save you a few steps," she said. "It wasn't too hard, even though I haven't been in any kind of library since high school."

"You already got the book? You know, it's too bad you never went to college. You've got a good knack for research."

This statement caught her off guard. Deep inside, she knew Sam would never belittle her despite her lack of higher education, but the comment stung just a bit. She had always regretted missing out while she wasted time on a useless first marriage. After that, she involved herself in helping her family because, as they got older, they couldn't run the café without her.

She decided on a gentle quip in response. "Yeah, but then again, you've got a college degree and you're working for *me*...in *my* café."

Sam realized he had made a mistake and took her hand. "Aw, I didn't mean it like that. You are the smartest and most capable woman I know."

"And spiteful, don't forget spiteful."

"How could I forget that?"

"I won't let you. Anyway, I do feel bad that I missed out."

"Well, you've done all right for yourself."

"I have, haven't I? Well, let me know when you need something else."

"Let's see what we have here. Sit down and read along."

To her, everything they read seemed to be along the same lines as the information they'd already heard. "Looks to be more of what we know," she said.

"That's the size of it. We're looking for subtle differences at this point. For instance, this one mentions bandits, not Apaches." Sam followed a footnote to the bibliography. "Oh, this source is in Spanish."

"I can read a little Spanish. Maybe I can find something we could copy down. Wait, I saw a copy machine downstairs, can we make copies?"

"I'm sure we can pay for some."

"Write down the title and I'll look it up. Maybe they have it."

She returned to the catalog, found what she was looking for, and wrote down the location, which looked completely different from the others, so she returned it to Sam.

"I don't know where this one is," she said

He glanced at her notation. "Oh, it must be in their special collections. It is probably a rare book."

"Is that a problem?"

"It might be. It depends on their policies. All we can do is ask. I've done all I can do with these books. Like you said, it's just more of what we already know. Let's put these books on that shelving cart and go check it out."

"You don't have to put them back?"

He chuckled. "Naw, they prefer to do it. Lowly students can't be trusted to put books back in the right place."

Sam used his crutches as they approached the special collections room.

"Is your leg bothering you?" she asked.

"Not that much, but there is something I've learned since the accident," he said.

"What?"

"It never hurts to play for sympathy."

"You idiot. Well, okay, here we go."

After they had showed their IDs and checked in, the special collections librarian was very helpful. The book they wanted was very old, and she insisted on handling it herself. She was fluent in Spanish as well as English, and she quickly found the passage they were interested in and translated it for them.

"Reading Spanish from the nineteenth century is much like reading English of the same era. It has differences from modern speech, but we can understand it." She read through a stylish pair of glasses perched at the end of her nose. She looked over the rims at Sam. "This seems to be about some form of treasure. So, you're a treasure hunter?"

"I guess," he said. "Maybe a little. But right now, we have a friend who may be out looking for this particular treasure, and he's overdue."

"I see. Well, this recounts the testimony of a man named Diego Mendoza, who was the lone survivor of a party that was ambushed near the *Camino Real de Tierra Adentro*. They fought off some assailants and attempted to elude them by heading east from their route to seek refuge in some mountains. The next day they...I don't understand this reference...it sounds something like they settled in front of something he calls a saddle where they found a circle of rocks. They set up a camp to defend themselves and were under siege for about a week. They killed their own oxen for food and used the carts for wood. They buried their cargo of...ah, here's the good part...*plata y oro*."

"Silver and gold," Sam and Smidgeon replied in unison.

"Correct. It was buried beyond the circle of rocks. Because it was the feast day of St. Michael, Padre de la Garza blessed the location in the name of the archangel." She continued reading quietly. "The rest is about his survival when everyone else was killed." She frowned. "Apparently they tried to break out with their remaining horses and wagons under cover of night and followed a circuitous path for a day and a half before all but Diego Mendoza were killed and even he was injured and left for dead. He spent the rest of his life trying to find the location, but he never found the circle of rocks again."

"Sad, really," Smidgeon said.

"It is," the librarian added.

Sam said, "Everything in that story is part and parcel to every lost gold story I've ever heard. So it all centers on a circle of rocks."

The librarian again looked at Sam over the rim of her glasses. "Yes, and that saddle reference. That is very confusing to me."

"I get that one...it's an old way of explaining a particular landmark. Two hills or mountains with a dip between them, that looks like the front and back of a saddle when seen from the side."

"I see. Now it makes more sense."

"Of course, there's a problem with that sort of reference. We have no directional orientation. It might look like a saddle from one direction but not from any other direction."

The librarian returned to the pages and scanned the Spanish words. "I see no sense of north, south, east, or west," she said. "Except that they went east from their original path."

Sam told the librarian, "You've been an immense help, Mrs...?"

"Beatrice Welbourne. Please call me Bea. You can skip the Mrs...I've never married."

Smidgeon spoke up. "I don't know what we would have done without your help, Bea."

"This is what I do. Luckily it's quiet today. I'm happy I was of some assistance. I must say, all of this talk of lost treasure is quite interesting."

"It does have its moments." Smidgeon handed Bea one of her cards. "If you're ever in Van Horn, stop in. Best food in town."

"The Mossback Café," she read. "All right. I have a sister who lives near Fort Stockton, and I've passed by Van Horn a number of times. I just might do that."

On the way home, Smidgeon said, "So, do you think we can do anything with what we've found?"

"Maybe, but after we talk it over with the others, somebody will have to get out into the field and hunt for that circle of rocks."

"That somebody better not include you," she said.

Sam rubbed his leg. "Judging from how it feels right now, it won't be any time soon for me."

~ * ~

It was evident the stranger was looking for someone or something. Although sunglasses effectively covered his eyes, his head moved methodically as he glanced around the dining room.

Lance was standing behind the register. "Can I help you? You can sit anywhere you like."

"Looking for somebody."

Lance swept a hand at the empty dining room. "Ain't anybody in here but you and me."

"Looking for a girl by the name of Holly. Got information she was working here."

The stranger looked ominous in his dark glasses and dark clothing. He was big, about six-foot-two, but had a very pale complexion. Lance was debating whether he should call to her when she emerged from the kitchen and abruptly stopped.

"Oh," she said. "Earl."

"Hello, Holly."

"How'd you find me?"

"You've been calling a lot of people looking for Dave. It wasn't hard to figure out where you were."

"I'm not hiding. I was out of money and I needed to rest and think."

"Dave needs to see you."

"So he's with you?"

"I didn't say that."

"Where is he?"

"I can't say that either. He took something from me that I need back."

"I don't have anything of his."

"Where's his truck? He won't tell us."

"How would I know where his truck is? Listen, I spent weeks looking and didn't find a trace of him."

"How'd you end up here?"

"I knew the owner and asked her to let me work for a while. I ain't rich, Earl. People need money to live, right? Why don't you let Dave go and leave us alone?"

Lance had heard enough. "Now, look, I'm the manager here and she's got work to do. She's answered your questions, now why don't you just mosey on out the danged door and go someplace else."

Earl turned to him, and Lance could feel a burning glare even through the sunglasses.

"So you have him?" Holly asked, tears welling in her eyes.

"Ain't saying." He glanced toward Lance again.

"You git on, now. I'm fixing to call the cops."

Earl edged toward the door and said to Holly, "You think about what you might know. I'll be in touch. I guess I should remind you, don't call the cops. " He turned to Lance, "That goes for you, too, tough guy."

He left and got into a black sedan.

Lance went to the window with an order pad and squinted through the dust kicked up by the car speeding off. "Dang, I wish she'd pave this lot. Only got the first three letters, GBH. Black Ford LTD, New Mexico plates. Mule should be able to do something with that."

He returned to the register and threw the pad down. "Dang, girl, I thought I was going to have to pull out my piece!"

"Sorry, Lance."

"So I guess it's pretty obvious you know him."

"That was Earl. He's one of Dave's prison buddies. You know, one of the ones he was talking to before he disappeared."

"I bet I know what he's after."

"What?"

"That note we found in the truck."

"Oh, I didn't think of that."

"It couldn't be anything else."

"So if they have him, there'll be a lot more trouble for him if we bring in the cops. They know that."

"Likely means trouble for them, too, hence the implied threats to both of us."

Nine

The following Sunday, Sam was back at the register, and he bantered with customers about the luxury of being able to walk without crutches. In the mid-morning, Smidgeon left for church, leaving Sam to work alone in the dining room. The door opened, revealing a petite Hispanic woman who hesitated as she scanned the dining room until her dark eyes connected with Sam's. He almost poured coffee down his shirt as he paused in mid-sip. Her face seemed familiar at first, but he couldn't quite place it because he came across so many different people from all walks of life while working in the café,

"You're the one I'm looking for." Her voice was familiar as well.

A sudden clarity popped into Sam's head with a jolt and his mind danced around the same way a dog gets excited when it detects a familiar scent. He'd met her five years earlier in Fort Stockton at a gas station. She had translated for her aunt, an old *bruja*, who had given him a peculiar type of stone meant to be a talisman of good fortune. They both returned to visit him later to give him fair warning of a new peril the old woman had sensed. That young girl had grown into an attractive young woman. Sam reasoned that she must be at least eighteen, but she looked older.

"You're ..." and in that instant he realized he never knew the young woman's name. "You...you came here with your aunt, the old woman."

"Yes. Sadly, *mi tia* is no longer with us."

"Oh. I'm so sorry."

"She lived a long life, *señor*." The girl smiled. "There is something you must know. She was more than *mi tia*, she was also my teacher and she has passed everything to me. Before she died, she reminded me that I would need to return to you."

"Why?"

"The stone was bonded between *tia* Asminda and you. Now its powers must be bonded to me...to both of us."

"Her name was Asminda?"

"Yes. And I am Ximena."

The intensity of her eyes burned a spot into his soul as she stared at him. Sam stammered, "S-so you're also a...?"

Ximena interrupted. "Please understand there are forces that must be returned to a certain balance, *señor*. You were recently in an accident? *Si*?"

"Yes," he said as he limped around the counter. "I broke my leg in an accident about a month ago."

"This is when *Tia* Asminda died."

Sam gulped.

"Her power could no longer protect you. She grasped my hands with the fire of her bond to you still burning in her soul and told me I must find you and renew the bond to protect you. Her fire now burns through me." She looked Sam up and down. "But...*it* is not here."

"No, it's at the house."

"You must get it."

"I can't leave now. I have to work."

"Then I will wait," she said, and she found a seat at a corner table.

Sam followed her. "Do you want some coffee and something to eat?"

"I have no money."

"Don't worry about it," Sam said. "Listen, my name is Sam. I don't know if I ever told you that."

"No, you did not, but *Tia* Asminda told me your name a long time ago. She saw it when she first touched your soul."

Sam felt his face flush.

In the kitchen he asked Lance, "Can you put a slice of that Saturday Morning Coffee Cake on a plate?"

"Sure thing, no ticket?"

"Naw, just an old friend. Remember the Mexican sorceress I told you about?"

"You mean the *bruja* who gave you that crazy good luck piece?"

"Yes. Her niece is here, all grown up. She wants to see that stone."

"You're kidding."

"No, I'm not. The old woman died, and Ximena is her replacement. She said the old woman asked her to find me."

"How did you say that name? Hih-men-a?"

"That's how she pronounced it."

"Wow, that's a witchy sort of name. Let me take the food out there. I want to see her." Lance was holding a plate with the coffeecake.

"Okay, sure."

Lance grabbed some wrapped silverware on the way to the table. Ximena's eyes met his and she smiled. "You are Sam's friend. I see that. If you are his friend, you are my friend as well. Thank you."

"You're welcome. I'm Lance." He extended his hand and his knees almost buckled when she touched him.

She smiled and repeated, "Lance. It's a good name for you. I like it."

Sam followed with a cup of coffee. "Do you need cream?"

"No," she said as she delicately picked at her food.

Sam and Lance returned to the kitchen.

"You didn't say she was beautiful!"

Sam laughed. "Yeah, she's pretty. But be careful, buddy, I think she's also a witch."

"How long is she here for?"

"I have no idea, but I need to go to the house at some point to retrieve that stone."

"Really? Why?"

"It's the reason she's here. Something about bonding its power to her now that her aunt is gone. She knew about my accident and said it was because the stone lost the old woman's protection when she died."

"Okay, then you better do it."

Sam glanced at a nearby clock. "I can't leave until Smidgeon gets back from church. She hates that stone, so she's not going to be too thrilled to hear Ximena's visit is about that thing."

They heard the dining room door open and close. Sam looked out and saw some people coming in.

"Okay, customers. I've got to get back to work."

Sam was aware of Ximena's stare while he followed with his normal restaurant routine. He noticed she ate slowly and with purpose. The slice of coffeecake was only half-consumed by the time Smidgeon arrived.

She noticed Ximena right away. She jerked her chin toward the table. "Who's that?" Sam led her into the kitchen.

"Her name is Ximena. She's the new *bruja* in town."

"That girl? She can't even be twenty."

"Her aunt gave me that stone, the good luck piece. She said she needs to see it and do something with it because her aunt died and now she has the power."

"Sam, you know how much I hate all this hooey."

"I know, yet she knew I'd been in an accident."

"You limp, honey."

"She said it before she saw me limp. According to her, the accident happened about the same time the old woman died. Ximena seems to think *that's* why I got hurt."

"So? What now?"

"I need to get the stone."

Smidgeon took a deep breath. "I guess the sooner she does whatever she needs to do, the sooner she can get out of here."

Lance brought Smidgeon a cup of coffee. "What? She has to leave?"

Sam smiled. "I think Lance here is a bit smitten with her."

She scowled at Lance. "Great. And I guess you gave her that coffeecake she's eating for free?"

"Sam did."

"She said she has no money."

"Lordy, another charity case. All right." She handed Sam her keys. "Go get your stupid stone and come right back so she can do whatever it is she wants to do. Hopefully she'll leave and that will be the last of her."

85

"I hope not," Lance said, ducking because Smidgeon threw a wadded up towel.

Sam went out through the back door and Lance returned to the grill.

"I guess I better go introduce myself," Smidgeon said.

Ximena stood as she approached, and extended her hand. "You are with Sam?"

"Smidgeon. This is my place."

"Of course. I am Ximena. I am pleased to meet any friend of Sam."

"So, where do you live, Ximena?"

"I stay with family here and there when I can. I used to drive *mi tia* to these places so she could do her work."

"And now you do her work."

"Yes. A *bruja* can be many things, but there is one thing I am not...I am not evil. Please understand that. I help people."

"You speak very good English, Ximena."

"I am American. It is true my family is from Mexico, but I grew up here, going to school, watching the television."

"Yet you say you are a *bruja*."

"It is not a choice I made; I was born to it."

Lance emerged from the kitchen and started a pot of fresh coffee, then returned to the kitchen. He frequently glanced at Ximena while she was talking to Smidgeon.

"This Lance...he is your friend, too?"

"He works here, but, yes, he's a friend, too."

"He is good."

"Yes, he's good."

"I mean, deep inside, he is a good man. I see it."

"I see it, too, honey. Do you want anything else? Sam has gone to get your stone."

"It is *his* stone. I am just an instrument of its influence on his fate." She hesitated. "Ah, you do not believe."

"No, and I don't like it."

"It has helped him."

"It has almost gotten him killed...several times."

"It has *saved* him. You are afraid. It is only natural to be afraid of things you do not understand."

"Look, do you want something else to eat or more coffee?"

Ximena pinched off another piece of her coffeecake. "This is very good. What do you call it?"

"That's our Saturday Morning Coffeecake."

"But it is Sunday."

"Well, we serve it both Saturday and Sunday."

"I like it. I like you, too. You are good."

"Yeah, I know, you can see it."

Ximena smiled as her eyes glowed back at Smidgeon. "Yes, I do see it."

Smidgeon felt a chill run down her spine.

"So you want some more coffeecake?"

"Yes, perhaps a small piece. Thank you."

While Smidgeon was cutting the coffeecake, Sam returned and she handed him the plate, saying with a smirk, "Here, you can take this out to your girlfriend. She said she likes it."

"You talked to her?"

"I did. She spouted more of her mumbo jumbo at me." Then Smidgeon's features softened. "Aw, I guess she's okay. Kinda sweet, really, in a creepy sort of way. Go do what you need to do, but don't let her scare the customers."

Lance was looking out the kitchen door window as Sam approached him from behind.

"Quit staring at her, Lance."

"I can't help it. I've never met anyone like her."

"Well, you need to get out of my way."

Lance stepped back and Sam returned to Ximena, sitting across the table from her. Only one other couple was in the dining room.

"Ah, you have the stone, and more of that wonderful coffee cake for me. It is a bit like *pan dulce*."

"Yes, I suppose it is."

"Hold the stone in your hand and make a fist."

Sam glanced at the other customers. "Here? Now?"

"*Si*. Do not worry about them; they will pay no notice. Please do it. A fist."

"Which one?"

"It doesn't matter." Sam complied, then she continued, "Now, extend both of your arms across the table toward me."

He followed her instructions and she suddenly grabbed his wrists with both of her hands and her eyes rolled up under her eyelids. Her fingers and palms suddenly burned against his skin with an intensity that made his heart race. Then, just as suddenly, her hands returned to normal.

"It is done."

"That's it?"

"Yes. Simple, no?" She glanced to the side. "See, they did not care."

"Easy." Sam found he was almost out of breath. "Now where do you go?"

"I have no place special. I like it here. What do you call this place?" She waved her hand in a wide arc.

"Van Horn?"

"Yes, Van Horn. I will stay here for some time. People will find me and give me money for helping them."

"Do you need money from me?"

She blushed and lowered her eyes. "No, *señor* Sam, you are special."

Sam stood. "Well, enjoy your coffeecake," he said, taking the first plate into the kitchen.

"Sam, your face is flushed," Smidgeon said.

"It's over," he said.

"She's leaving?"

"No. She said she was staying here."

Smidgeon's eyes widened. "In the café?"

"No, in town."

"Where?"

"She wasn't specific."

"Well, I'm glad," Lance remarked as he flipped a burger on the grill.

"You leave that girl alone," Smidgeon said, "She young enough to be..."

The kitchen door suddenly squeaked open and they turned to see Ximena standing there.

"*Señor* Sam!"

"Yes?"

"I've just seen something else. You are *all* in danger." She pointed at each of them in turn as she said, "All of you. Others, too. This is why I need to stay close."

"When did you see this?"

"Right now. As soon as the stone bonded with me, I could see it...a shadow of great danger surrounds you all. *Cuidado!* I must leave now, but I will be near and will see you soon." She handed Sam her empty plate, turned and left. They heard the front door a few seconds later.

Sam glanced at Smidgeon and she glared back, so he looked over at Lance and could tell he was spellbound.

Sam asked, "Well, it's nothing we didn't already know, right? Except *Cuidado*. Anybody know what that means?"

Smidgeon placed her hands on her hips and continued glowering at Sam. "It was good advice for you in more ways than one. It means watch out, you know, like beware."

"Right," he said.

Smidgeon continued. "Everything is just peachy. And *you*," she said to Lance, "you can just get that bee right out of your bonnet!"

Ten

Mule ended a call and leaned back in his chair. After a few minutes of contemplation, he sat forward and rummaged through the notes scattered around his desktop until he found a small notepad and jotted something down. "I feel guilty, taking new paying jobs when I figure I should be chasing Holly's boyfriend."

Lance called out from the living room. "You're talking to yourself again, man...and, anyway, don't you need paying jobs?"

Mule entered the living room. "You eavesdropping again?"

"Sorry, man, I suppose it's one of the problems with being roomies. Besides, you talk loud, even to yourself."

"I guess I am guilty of that, and yes, I do need paying jobs. I don't want to end up slinging hash like you."

"Aw, man."

They both laughed and Mule settled onto the couch next to Lance. "What are you doing out here?"

"Just sitting. I can't get Ximena out of my head."

"Oh, that gal you ran into at the café?"

Lance lowered his head. "She's beautiful, man."

"If you're this goofy over her, I'm sure she must be breathtaking."

"What kind of jobs you getting?"

"Two philandering husbands and one philandering wife."

"Three in one day in this small town?"

"Well, one in Marfa."

"You're the one who decided to come here because there were no PIs. Isn't that the key to success in business, find a need and fill it?"

"I guess so. Oh, I also got a call about that black LTD you asked me about. Only one hit on that model with those first three letters. They matched a car stolen from Roswell."

"Figures," Lance said.

"Actually, it does. It tells us it is likely the right car. Tough guy making trouble...stolen car. It adds up."

"So we can get the police looking for a stolen car."

"I did that, and the car's already turned up. It was abandoned near Carlsbad."

"Oh, use it and lose it."

"Exactly, and by my way of figuring, they probably stole another one. They think they're being clever, but they're leaving a trail. It's just a matter of time before this guy or somebody he works with comes back down here to cause more trouble."

"They ain't getting nothing."

"Of course not. But we don't want to wait, so either one or both of us should head back up to New Mexico and do more snooping around. Plus, we have the additional information Sam and Smidgeon found at the library."

"So we just snooping, or are we hiking, too?"

"Well, you know I can't manage the hiking."

"But I can," Lance said. "Might help take my mind off of other things."

~ * ~

Sam locked the door at closing time but paused when he saw a familiar Olds pull into the parking lot. He unlocked the door and opened it.

"You're running a little late, aren't you, Mule?"

"Wanted to talk to you about a couple of things, if'n you don't mind."

"Sure, come on in. Everything's put away, but if you're hungry I could maybe rustle up a sandwich."

"That's tempting, but I'm okay."

Sam relocked the door, and they sat at the nearest table.

"Lance wants to go back to New Mexico to look for that stupid treasure."

"I'm not surprised. If I was healthy, I'd already be out there."

"You're both a couple of idiots, you know that?"

Sam laughed. "Don't worry about me. I'm under strict orders to ignore those kind of thoughts."

"Doctor's orders?"

Sam shook his head. "No, Smidgeon's."

"My advice is to always abide by the counsel of a good woman. Which brings me to the second thing. Exactly who is this Ximena Lance keeps talking about?"

"That's hard to explain. She's a young woman who says she's a *bruja*. She showed up here the other day." Sam decided to defer the rest of his history with her.

"So you're saying she's a witch? I can't say I believe in that hogwash but, you know, there was one who passed through Colorado City a while back when I was a cop. I heard some pretty outlandish stories about that one. So you think she's maybe cast a spell on him or something?"

"I'm not sure what you mean. You think she cast a spell on Lance?"

"He is obsessed with her. He talks about her all the time."

"I know he was attracted to her, but I warned him she's pretty young for him."

"Did she return his attention?"

"Not that I could tell. We only saw her that one time."

"He told me you knew her; she came to see you."

Sam took in a deep breath. "I've met her twice. Both times she was with her aunt. *She* was the *bruja*, but it was more likely she was a great-aunt because she seemed pretty old. She sensed something about me, trouble she said, and gave me a good luck piece. There was definitely some strangeness there, but who am I to judge? Then again, I'm still alive, so who knows? Maybe it worked. Anyway, Ximena told me her aunt had died and that she was now the *bruja*."

"So she came here specifically to see you."

"Yeah. Something about bonding the good luck charm to her. She said that was likely why I got hurt...the old woman had died and I had lost the protection."

"Don't that beat all." Mule chuckled. "Do you believe in this stuff?"

"All I know is...there have been several times I could have died in the last five years but here I am, still alive."

"Well, I'm just concerned about Lance. One, he don't need to go off into the unknown on any treasure hunt, and two, especially not when his judgment is clouded by his feelings for this young lady."

"Agreed."

When Sam got home, he shared Mule's concerns with Smidgeon.

"Oh, my," she said. "This afternoon he asked for a few more days off, and I told him it was okay."

Sam frowned. "I don't like it, but he's a grown man. We can't forbid him from going."

"He's going to need some of your equipment, though."

"Yeah, but I've already told him he could borrow it, so I can't suddenly tell him no."

"Let me think about what we can do about it. Maybe I can delay him a bit."

"Why, when was he talking about going?"

"Day after tomorrow."

"I don't know what the hurry is; we know Dave isn't out there."

"Correction, it looks like maybe he isn't, but we don't know if that guy was on the level. Look, I'll see if I can claim the schedule won't allow it for a few days."

"He's too smart to believe that."

"What else can we do?"

"I really don't know."

~ * ~

Lance emerged from a small store and stopped abruptly. Ximena was standing by his truck.

"Hello, Mr. Lance."

He managed to stammer, "Ximena?"

"Of course."

She blinked her brown eyes rapidly several times and Lance felt his knees go weak. He put the sack of groceries in the bed of his truck.

Her gaze locked on his and she said, "I have been thinking about you ever since we met. Can we talk?"

"Here? Or did you want to go someplace?"

She pointed to a station wagon not far from his truck.

"Please, come sit with me in my car."

As he walked around the outside of the car, he could see she had the back of it outfitted with a sleeping bag.

He stared out the windshield from the passenger seat and asked, "You sleep in here?"

"Yes, sometimes." She rested her hands on the steering wheel.

"Is it safe?"

"I am not afraid. *Mi tia abuela* taught me many ways of protection." Ximena lowered her eyes. "I must confess, I have many feelings about you."

His heart pounded. "I...I like you, Ximena."

"That is one of the feelings I have...another is great danger. I am fearful because something evil threatens you." She looked back at him and his heart melted when he looked into her eyes. "Soon," she added.

"What is it?"

"I cannot see what it is, but I know it is there."

She took one hand off the steering wheel and grasped his hand. It felt very warm, almost hot.

She gasped and released his hand.

"It is stronger now."

She fumbled with the bag on her lap and pulled out a small yellow and green piece of stone. "Take this, then make fists with both of your hands!"

Lance did what he was told and she turned toward him. "Hold out your arms now."

She held onto his wrists tightly and her hands were so hot he thought for sure his flesh had burned. She released him and he could see his arms were fine. She was panting.

"Hold the stone tightly for as long as you can."

"What is it?"

"It is your protection." She leaned forward and kissed Lance on the cheek. "It binds you to me as well."

"Ximena..."

"Enough! I must be on my way. I know your feelings for me...I know many things about you, but we must both be strong until we fight away this evil. We cannot let our feelings confuse our minds. Keep that stone close to you. If you need my help, I will know it and I will find you. Now, I must leave."

"But..."

"Do what I say." She smiled and blinked again, then touched his cheek where she had kissed it. "Now, please go."

He got out of the car and she drove off without looking back at him. He imagined he could still feel the softness of her lips on his cheek. He looked down at his hand. His fist still squeezed the stone and it was beginning to ache because he was clutching it so tightly. He slowly opened his fingers and held it up to his face. "Odd coloring," he said, and he stashed it in the small watch pocket of his jeans and scanned his surroundings before heading back to his truck.

"Don't see no danger around here, but I'm not about to take her warning lightly."

At home, he opened the door and was greeted by Prewash. "Come on, girl, I know you need to go out." She stood in the doorway and stared at him, as if she sensed something different. "Come on, do you need to go out or not?"

She gingerly made her way down the steps, then paused at his feet. She raised on her hind legs and sniffed at his watch pocket.

"Oh, so you know about that, huh? I should have figured you'd be working in cahoots with her."

With that, Prewash bounded off and proceeded to take care of her other business.

Lance could see Mule's car was gone and when he went back inside, he found a note. He read it and then dropped it to the table exclaiming, "He went to New Mexico without me!"

He called the café and Sam answered.

"Hey, you know anything about Mule heading off to New Mexico? He left me a note."

"No, he said he was worried about you going off without *him*, but he didn't mention anything about taking off alone."

"I hope he's not high-tailing it out into that wilderness."

"Like he thought you were planning to do?"

"Yeah, but I'm younger and know more of what I'm doing."

"He doesn't seem like the type, and he doesn't have any equipment for that sort of thing. At least he didn't borrow any from me. Something else must have come up. Look, based on what that guy said to you and Holly, we don't think Dave is out there anyway. I'm thinking if that dude comes back, we just give him the note. We can copy it down and still basically have it. Then maybe he'll leave Holly alone."

"I don't know about that. I really think there is more to this story and it all hinges on what's out in the desert," Lance said. "Oh, I ran into that Ximena girl again."

"Really?"

"I'd dropped by the store on the way home and she was waiting outside my truck in the parking lot. She wanted to tell me I was in danger."

"She already told us that the other day, remember?"

"She seemed more emphatic this time. And she gave me a special little stone, just like her aunt did with you."

"Knowing what I know now, I'd take that seriously."

"Don't think I'm not. And I think she likes me, Sam. I really do."

"I know you like her. Maybe she's just like the rest of us, and doesn't want anything bad to happen to you."

"Could be. And perhaps she's right about the danger, too. I reckon maybe Mule taking off without me is a good thing. I guess I'll just wait to hear from him. Tell Smidgeon I'm not taking off after all."

"I will. Is that all Ximena wanted?"

"She said we must deal with this evil first before we explore anything else between us."

"Just remember, she's young, Lance." Sam chuckled as he added, "Oh, and she's a witch."

"Does that matter?"

"I don't know if it does or not. I just wanted to remind you in case it does."

~ * ~

Mule sped north thinking about his plan. "Finding Holly's boyfriend is what I'm supposed to be doing, so I'm going to follow up on that stolen car. I'm sure there was another theft close by," he mumbled to himself. "And if this little trip keeps Lance from getting himself into some fool's errand, all the better."

A few hours later, he pulled into the parking lot of the same restaurant in Roswell where he and Lance had met Detective Michaels. He asked inside for a phone book and looked up the Roswell PD.

"You can use our phone if it's local." It was the same waitress they'd talked to before.

"Much obliged." He dialed the number and asked for the detective.

"Detective, this is Mule Hollis."

"Oh, the PI from Texas, I remember. Do you have some information for me?"

"Some, but I'm looking to get more than give. Can I meet you? I'm at the café where we met."

"I can be there in five minutes."

Mule sat at a table and nursed a cup of coffee while he waited. He looked up when a familiar face appeared, and he waved to the empty seat across from him. Michaels reached out and shook Mule's hand as he sat.

"So what's up? We have nothing new on our end."

"A guy came by to see the girlfriend. He seemed to think she might have something Dave had taken from him."

"Really? Any idea who he was?"

"Somebody named Earl is all she said. He drove off in a black LTD. We got a partial New Mexico plate. A friend of mine in your state police matched it to a stolen LTD recovered in Carlsbad."

"Where was it stolen?"

"Roswell."

"Oh, I see, and you want to know more about it."

"Exactly. But it's a solid lead for you, too. Oh, I figure there was probably a fresh steal in Carlsbad at the same time. If so, there might..."

Michaels interrupted. "I'm way ahead of you...there might be a pattern."

"Yes. I'm thinking we can help each other."

"How so?"

"I'll keep nosing around and try to get more information, then you back it up with solid police work."

"That's not how we do things."

"Look, I'm doing a favor for a friend. I don't know that I'll be paid for my work but you're already being paid. And I have a hunch we've got something much bigger here than just a parole violation."

"I checked you out, Mule."

"Oh? And what did you find?"

"You used to be a cop yourself. You lost an election for sheriff against a colleague and, along with losing the election, you lost your job. That's got to be a rough way to retire."

"I've gotten used to it and I find I like the new pace."

"We could probably squeeze you in here."

"Well, that's interesting and it's tempting, but I have a job to do right now and I think working it benefits us both. What do you say?"

"Okay, I'll see what I can dig up. Where can I find you?"

"I'm heading up to Capitan. I'll be at the Smoky Bear Motel."

It was dark by the time Mule checked into his room. Thirty minutes after he got there, the phone rang.

"Mule?" The voice was familiar.

"Yeah."

"This is Detective Michaels. I've got something for you. I'm coming up there in the morning."

"This about the LTD?"

"Yeah, you were right, it was stolen from Roswell. No suspects. And you were right about something else, too...a car was stolen in Carlsbad the same day that car was abandoned."

"What kind of car was stolen in Carlsbad?"

"Dark green Mercury, 1982 model."

"Interesting."

"It had New York plates, but there was another theft, too...a set of New Mexico plates. Same parking lot."

"We have that number?"

"Like I said, I'll be up early in the morning. I'll call when I get there."

Eleven

Sam sat on the couch gently caressing MamaKat as he passed another sleepless night in the dark living room. The cat suddenly ceased her purring, tensed, then growled and hissed. A faint glow appeared on the other end of the couch and the image of Loot materialized.

"'Morning, Sam."

"Geez, you about gave me a heart attack...you even scared the cat. Can't you warn me or something?"

"I'd do it if I could, Sam, but you know this takes a lot of effort."

"I'm sorry. You popping up like that just startled me. What's up?"

"There's something fishy about these women who've come around. I can't quite put my finger on it yet, but I got me a feeling."

"Well, they both seem pretty harmless to us."

"Just be careful."

"I always am..."

With that, the image faded.

A moment later he was surprised again.

"Who are you talking to?"

Sam looked up and saw Smidgeon wearily leaning against the hallway doorframe.

"Just mumbling to myself."

"It sounded like you were having a conversation. Were you on the phone?"

"Phone's over there," he said, pointing across the room.

She walked over and snuggled next to him on the couch. "You'd tell me if it was something else, wouldn't you?" She tipped Sam's chin toward her, stretched her lips up and kissed him.

His heart began to race. He hated deceiving Smidgeon. "What do you remember about that night out in the field?"

"Oh, when we were chasing that murderer?"

"Yes."

"I remember a hazy sort of light, and you blurted out Loot's name. Why?"

"What would you say if I told you I think I saw him?"

"Sam, you know I don't hold with that sort of thing."

"Give me a straight answer."

"Okay, at the time I thought for just a second it looked a little like Loot, but I put the notion right out of my mind because it just didn't make sense."

"Didn't it?"

"I kind of figured it was the power of suggestion...you said Loot, so I was trying to see what you thought you saw. What are you saying...that we saw his ghost?" She sat upright and looked him in the eye. "Wait, were you just..."

"He's shows up every now and then. I think he follows me."

"Loot follows you."

"I know it sounds strange."

She nestled back against his shoulder. "And I guess you have conversations with him?"

"Short ones. He can't appear for very long."

"Is that what you were just doing?"

Sam whispered, "Yeah."

Smidgeon looked around the room.

"Is he here now, watching us? Does he watch us, you know, *all* the time?"

"I don't think it works like that."

"I hope not because I gotta tell you, even the thought of that really gives me the heebie-jeebies." She bunched up the front of her robe, holding it together near her chin.

"I thought it was unsettling at first, too."

"So what does he say?"

"This time, he told me to watch out for both Holly and Ximena because he has an uneasy feeling about them. He doesn't know why."

"Oh, well, that's easy to explain. I have an uneasy feeling about them, too. You say you have a ghost, but I have a woman's intuition and I think that trumps your ghost. Come on, let's go back to bed."

Sam followed her down the hallway. She paused and turned around. "You sure he's not following us?"

"I don't see him right now."

She raised on her tiptoes and kissed him. "He better not, 'cause I don't want him to see what happens next."

~ * ~

Mule Hollis sat alone in his motel room watching the morning news. The sudden ringing of the phone momentarily drowned out the program.

"Hello?"

"Mule. Michaels here. I'm down in the restaurant. Are you up?"

"Been waiting for your call. I'll be right down."

He glanced at his watch and mumbled, "Seven-thirty, he didn't waste much time...but I'm glad. I'm ready for some coffee."

Mule made the short walk to the café and paused to look around after he entered. He saw Michaels in the corner booth and sat down.

"When you said early, you meant it."

"Early bird, right? So where's your sidekick?"

"Lance? Back in Texas. I decided I could cover more ground on my own this trip."

"So I did some checking. I figure this Earl character you mentioned is Earl Rector. He's a recently paroled former resident of the same institution where David Adams served his sentence. Among Rector's many talents is car theft. In the past, he's been known to work for a local crime boss, Rey Mendoza."

"He needs, he sees, he steals."

"Yeah, that's about the size of it. These look like short term thefts."

"Like he's covering his tracks."

"That's what I think. There's already a warrant for him, too, for parole violation. He's AWOL with his parole officer."

"About par for the course, I'd say." Mule sipped his coffee.

"So, what are you looking for around here? I assume Dave Adams' truck was towed here, but I thought you already checked on that. I heard they found a handgun in it. Was that you?"

"Ain't saying," Mule said.

"I guess it doesn't matter who found it; that's a parole violation for David Adams."

"It might stick, but no way to prove it was his."

"You know the drill...his car, his gun. So, what's the connection between these two and the area around Arabela and Capitan?"

"That's the big question. According to Holly Slidell, it all has to do with something called Archangel."

"Oh, you mean the Archangel Cache? Over the years, we've seen a lot of people go missing looking for that. It's an old legend and I think it's really pretty silly. If it ever existed, it was probably plundered a long time ago."

"That's the story with most so-called hidden treasures."

"So you think he parked to go hiking into the Capitan Mountains to look for it?"

"If that were the case, I doubt he would have parked it where it was found. Lance figured out there was damage to the oil pan of the truck. We think he got out to check the car while he was scouting. I assume he was waylaid after he stopped."

"Wait, are you suggesting Earl Rector followed him and kidnapped him?"

"No way of telling, but that would be my guess."

"Why didn't you tell me this yesterday? We could have been looking."

"It's just a theory; there isn't any proof. The vehicles are the only clues and they don't tell us much. That and the fact that Earl came to see Holly. We need to find the second car, even though all that will probably lead to is another stolen car."

"No doubt."

"So, why are you here in Capitan?"

"It's a good central base if they are operating here in Lincoln County. There's a local expert on the Archangel Cache, too. We talked to him last time we were here. I reckon I might see if I can glean anything more from him."

"Well, there is a lot of desert out there for them to get lost in." Michaels finished his coffee and waved for the check.

~ * ~

Smidgeon hurried to the register to answer the phone.

"Mossback."

"I'm looking for Smidgeon Toll."

"You've found her."

"This is Bea Welbourne, we spoke recently..."

"Oh, from the library. Right. What can I do for you?"

"I was fascinated by your investigations and decided to dig a little deeper."

"Oh, you didn't have to do that."

"I confess I dabble in mystery writing. Nothing published as yet, but research is a big part of what I do. My brother was something of a treasure hunter before he died and because of that, these kinds of stories always fascinate me."

"What did you find?"

"Several more accounts of Diego Mendoza. I thought I might come down there this weekend and share them with you. Will you and Sam be able to spare me some time?"

"Most Saturday afternoons are dead here, so come on down."

"I'm intrigued by the name of your café as well, so I'll be thrilled at the chance to see it."

"Well, it ain't much, but it's home. So I guess we'll see you Saturday?"

"Yes, I'll see you then. Bye now."

"Bye." Smidgeon put the phone down and stared out the window for a moment, lost in thought.

"Who was that?" Sam asked. He and Lance had been busing tables and stopped to listen when they heard Smidgeon's side of the phone conversation.

"Bea Welbourne, you know, the librarian we talked to in El Paso. She has more information."

"Did she say what it was?"

"She's coming down here this weekend to tell us. I guess it was more than she wanted to say over the phone."

Sam turned to Lance. "Good thing you didn't go out there. In my experience, the more information we can accumulate, the better off we are in the long run."

Lance lowered his eyes. "You're probably right. Hey, did you tell Smidgeon about the truck?"

"What truck?" Smidgeon asked.

"Loot's old Jeep," Lance said.

"We were just talking in the kitchen. Lance says I should start driving it since my VW was totaled."

"Don't forget, the truck's yours," Lance said, adding, "it's been parked at the house all this time, but Loot left it to you."

"It's a piece of junk," Smidgeon said. "Besides, are you cleared to drive?"

"Doc said I can do anything within reason, the reason being pain. If it hurts, don't do it."

"That's a standard. You think you can push in the clutch with your hurt leg?"

"It's feeling pretty good. I get a twinge every now and then, but all I can do is try it."

She sighed. "I know better than to try to stop you. If you can drive that thing without hurting your leg, then I'm fine with it. But you ain't driving it to any doctor appointments in El Paso."

Sam said, "Just local, I promise."

~ * ~

Blalock's Curios' open sign was visible through the dingy window, so Mule opened the door and walked in.

"Howdy! Mule, wasn't it?"

108

"Yes. How're you doing, Mitch?"

He chortled and waved a hand around. "Really busy, as you can see. What can I do for you?"

"Maybe answer a few more questions."

"About the Archangel Cache?"

"Yeah. We read a little more about the *Camino Real de Tierra Adentro*. You told us that's the trail they were following when they were attacked, right?"

"Right. That actually is one of the problems with the stories. It doesn't follow that they'd come this far east from the *Camino Real*. It's one reason I not sure it is even in the Capitans."

"You didn't say *that* when we were here."

"That's because when somebody's here spending money in our local economy, it doesn't pay to send people anyplace else."

Mule sighed. "You business people are all alike."

"Hey, we need to make a living just like you do. You sell yourself, you know, your services, don't you, mister private investigator?"

"I don't deceive people to make extra money."

Mitch waved his arm in another arc. "See any customers? This is a tough place to make a living."

"I get that. I didn't come here to put you on the defensive. I don't care how you treat the rubes, but I'm not one of them. A man is missing and I'm trying to find him."

"Well, like I said, the location doesn't quite fit the standard stories."

"So where else could it be?"

"Could be just about anywhere."

"Okay, then, I guess I've found out what I wanted to know."

"Maybe if you bought something."

Mule laughed. "You really take the cake."

"Look, I haven't made a sale all day. I've given you everything you've asked for, and for nothing. Say, I've got some nice crystals over there." He pointed to a row of glass display cases. One case glowed purple with the unmistakable signature of a black light and several stones glowing with a distinctive green caught his eye.

"What are those, the greenish ones?"

"Ah, good eye. Mexican adamite. They fluoresce very nicely, don't they?" Mitch grabbed the brightest one out of the case. "Twenty bucks for you. It's a bargain."

Mule pulled a twenty out of his wallet. "Twenty, tax included."

"Sure. Tax included."

"So, we square?"

Mitch nodded and Mule pocketed the stone and left the store.

"This trip has been kind of a waste," he said to himself as he began to drive. "Guess I'll head back home and hope Michaels comes up with something on either Earl Rector or that car."

A little after sunset, he pulled up to the house. Lance's truck was in the drive. The shed was open, and he could see that the old Jeep truck was missing.

Inside, Lance was emptying a can of dog food into a bowl for Prewash.

"So, you're back earlier than I thought you'd be."

"Sorry, I guess I didn't want you to go out there half-cocked and I'm glad I did. I think the entire Capitan thing might be a dead end."

"Why would you think that?"

"It's too far from the *Camino Real de Tierra Adentro*, that's why."

"How's that?"

"The stories say they were pursued by Apaches or bandits. How could they go that far if they were being attacked? It doesn't make sense. Mitch Blalock admitted he feels the same way."

"That's the opposite of what he said before."

"He claims he encourages people at first so they stick around and spend more money in town."

"Well, the librarian Sam and Smidgeon met in El Paso called the café today. She's coming here this weekend with some more information. She's been researching on her own."

"That's interesting. Maybe whatever she found will throw some new light on the problem."

"It was a long way to go to find basically nothing. Did you turn up *anything* else?"

"Yeah, I did get a little bit more. Holly's visitor is likely named Earl Rector, who is apparently a career criminal with a lot of experience stealing cars. He most likely works for a criminal gang run by a guy named Rey Mendoza. Oh, and there's this," Mule said, as he pulled the piece of stone from his pocket and handed it to Lance. "Blalock called it Mexican adamite. He insisted I buy something from him. I'm no stranger to paying for information, so I figured it was the least I could do, even though he was not nearly as talkative this trip."

"Wow!" Lance said as he turned the stone in his hands. "This is really intriguing."

"Yeah, I thought it was kind of interesting. It glows under a black light."

"It's not just that," Lance said, handing the stone back to Mule. "Look at this," he said, and he fished the stone Ximena had given him out of his watch pocket.

Mule held it up to the light and examined it closely. "I'd say it's the same thing...Mexican adamite."

"Ximena gave it to me as a sort of good luck charm."

"You were right, it really is an intriguing coincidence," Mule said.

"Wait, I just realized...it's adamite?" Lance added, "Don't forget, we're looking for a guy named Adams."

"I didn't even make that connection."

"Pretty wild stuff," Lance said.

Twelve

On Saturday, Sam, Smidgeon, Holly, and Lance took advantage of a slack period and sat down to eat a late lunch together. They all looked at each other when they heard a car in the parking lot.

"Never fails," Sam said. "We just sit down to eat and here come some customers."

"Hey, don't complain...it's good for business," Lance said, as he grabbed his plate and headed into the kitchen. "I guess I'll have to eat on the run."

Sam and Smidgeon recognized her the moment she walked in. The woman was casually dressed, but she was unmistakably the same woman they had last seen wearing staid professional attire in the library.

"Bea!"

"Hello, Smidgeon. I made good time, but it's a relief to get off the road. I visit my sister often enough, so I should be used to this ride but it tends to be tedious." She dropped her purse on the table and scrutinized her surroundings. "So this is The Mossback Café."

"This is it. Are you hungry?"

"Not yet, I need a few minutes to get situated, but some coffee would be great."

Sam limped over to the drink station and returned with a steaming cup. "Cream?"

"No, I like it black."

Lance returned from the kitchen with his plate. "Guess I can eat out here after all."

Smidgeon spoke up. "Y'all, this is Bea Welbourne, a librarian from the University of Texas El Paso. She helped us look up some stuff the last time we were there."

Bea sat and pulled a folder from her purse. She took a deep breath. "My, I didn't know there would be so many people."

"Oh, I'm sorry." Smidgeon pointed at each in turn. "You know Sam, and that is Holly, and this is Lance. Trust me, we are *all* interested in what you have to tell us. I just wish Mule was here."

"Mule?"

"He's a private investigator who's been working with us."

"I see."

"He's out on a case," Lance said. "Cheating husband, I think. I can fill him in later."

Bea smiled. "Small town life, big city problems. Well, I'll get right to it then…I did some cross referencing and dug a little more into that incident we were researching when you visited, and I found something quite remarkable."

"You have our attention," Sam said.

"Mendoza's account says they were attacked by bandits. I saw this same explanation stated as fact in several sources, but then I discovered that his account is inaccurate."

"How so?" Sam asked.

"Although there were regular shipments along the *Camino Real de Tierra Adentro*, and we all naturally assumed, I guess along with almost everybody else through the years...everyone has assumed this was one of those shipments, but it turns out Mendoza and Padre de la Garza were, in fact, thieves who were trying to smuggle a hoard of riches back to Mexico. Their pursuers were soldiers sent to stop them."

"That was why they were so far off the main trail!" Lance exclaimed. "But who is this Mendoza you mentioned?"

Sam said, "Diego Mendoza was a member of the expedition that was attacked."

"Mule just told me about another guy with that same name. The tough guy who came to see Holly supposedly works for a Rey Mendoza."

"It's a fairly common name," Bea interjected.

"Still," Lance said, "makes me wonder if there's somehow a connection."

Bea glanced at the three friends in turn, then smiled and said, "And you wonder why this investigation has struck my fancy. Going on, I've translated and transcribed an official document I found that reports on the theft. The stolen articles were never recovered, but all of the thieves were caught and killed."

"All of them but one," Sam said. "Mendoza."

Bea smiled. "Perhaps." She shuffled her papers. "And I found something else very noteworthy."

Sam spoke up. "Wow. That's already pretty exciting. Their hiding stolen loot is so logical. It makes perfect sense."

"It does. I found it astounding that this account contradicts every other mention of this Saint Michael the Archangel treasure I could find. It seems this Padre de la

Garza dabbled in astronomy and knew an eclipse of the moon was predicted and, although their lair was fairly well defended, he thought they could use the temporary added darkness to cover their attempt to hide their purloined goods and make good their escape. It almost worked, too. They got some distance away before their pursuers caught them. Most were killed outright, but the good padre was captured alive. He was wounded but he lived long enough to be tortured in an attempt to force a confession. That's how they learned what he knew about the eclipse. But he refused to tell them exactly where the hoard was hidden. Before he died, he cursed them and cursed the eclipse for failing him. There was an interesting quote." She read directly from her notes. "He said they'd never find the treasure because Saint Michael's power was protecting it with something he called penumbra."

"Penumbra? Is that Spanish?" Sam asked.

"I wondered that, too, so I looked it up. It is the same in both English and Spanish. It's a Latin word that was incorporated into both languages intact." She continued slowly, "It is the partially shaded outer region of the shadow cast by an opaque object, and most commonly refers to the outer shadow of a lunar eclipse."

"So he violates the ten commandments by stealing, then tries to use his religion to compensate," Lance said. "That's messed up."

"So this account doesn't say anything about Mendoza?" Sam asked.

"No, they apparently didn't know about him, so his account seems to hold true. He was left for dead and woke up to find everyone around him dead and he managed to make his escape before daylight."

Smidgeon said, "I wonder why the hacienda he found didn't turn him in."

"They probably didn't know about the theft. News travelled slowly in those days," Lance said.

Sam said, "And I guess with the soldiers thinking everyone was dead, their account of the incident faded from history, at least except for Mendoza's biased story about his lost treasure."

Bea smiled. "That is probably a good guess. And, of course, he wouldn't tell anyone he was a thief. He'd tell anyone who would listen that he was just one more person ambushed by bandits. I found one other fascinating thing, an account written by Mendoza's son in the 1800s. Apparently he also fell under the spell of the treasure story."

Lance winked at Sam and said, "Gold fever."

"He claimed his father told him the cache was not buried within the circle of stones; it was taken to a protected place nearby. The words *arroyo* and *gruta* were both used in an unusual way. *Gruta* is Spanish for grotto, but a grotto doesn't seem to fit into my concept of an arroyo. Anyway, this detail was apparently confided to him by his father. Does it make sense to you, Sam?"

"Hmmm, I guess it could be an indentation or a cutout gouged in a side wall. If it were me looking, that is what I'd look for. Flash floods will do weird things to those walls over time."

"So it is not in the circle of stones, but it's close," Lance added.

"Right," Bea said.

"I can't believe you found all of this so quickly," Smidgeon said.

"It's what I do, day in, day out. My job is to make so-called smart professors look like geniuses."

Holly had remained quiet but broke her silence. "I'm not sure I understand most of what you've said. How is this supposed to help us find Dave? Sounds to me like you guys are ready to go treasure hunting for yourselves."

"If this is what Dave was after, it helps put us on his trail," Sam said.

"So this helps?" Bea asked.

"You done good," Lance answered. "I almost went out there again the other day. This adds a lot more perspective. Now we need to figure out if there's a connection to this Rey Mendoza guy."

"I'll keep looking around whenever I have a chance," she said. "It was serendipitous in a way. I was looking for something else and happened across a document that gave a clue to the report I found. I'm happy to help. This is much more fulfilling than pure academic research."

"That is often the case," Sam said.

Bea turned to him. "So you've done this type of research before?"

"A little, as an undergraduate. One reference leads to another reference...and sometimes a third and then you get sidetracked by something else."

"Exactly. Now, before I head out to my sister's place in Forth Stockton, what about that bite to eat? I've been smelling good things the entire time I've been talking and I've decided I better eat!"

"Holly, grab Bea a menu. You want some more coffee?"

"Yes, thank you so much."

"We need to be thanking *you*," Sam said.

~ * ~

Mule was working at his desk when the phone rang. "Mule Hollis."

"Michaels here. Glad I caught you. I hoped you were back in your office. I picked up some more information on Earl Rector. It turns out he's got a buddy named Ding Stewart and we're pretty sure they're working together."

"Ding?"

"Believe it or not, that's his real name."

"What were his parents thinking?"

"I quit being amazed by given names a long time ago. Ding did time along with Earl and Dave...and he got out not long after they did."

"What is Ding into?"

"Just about everything. Like Earl, he's got a rap sheet about a mile long. They both are probably working for that Rey Mendoza I told you about, but I haven't been able to nail that down for sure yet."

"So these guys enlisted David Adams for some help in whatever caper their unknown third party is up to. It's a good way to muddy the trail."

"That would be my guess. Anyway, I better get back to it. Call me if you dig up anything we can use, Mule."

"I will. Thanks for the heads up."

Later that evening, Lance brought some food home from the café.

"I'm glad I like that danged café's food," Mule said. "It seems to be most of what we eat."

"Well, I've been cooking all day and usually get home late, so the last thing I want to do is more cooking."

"Saves us on groceries, though. Oh, by the way, I found out our friend Earl has a partner in crime, Ding Stewart."

"Ding?" Lance asked.

"That's his name. Detective Michaels thinks they both work for that Rey Mendoza fellow."

Lance leaned forward and said, "You know, there's a Diego Mendoza attached to the original Archangel Cache mystery. Turns out he was a bit into criminal mischief himself."

"Two Mendozas? Well it might be a coincidence but then again..."

Their conversation was interrupted by a faint knock on the front door.

"I'll get it," Lance said. Prewash followed closely, but cowered behind his leg as he approached the door. He eyed the shotgun leaning to the side but decided to take his chances and threw the door open. His heart immediately began thumping rapidly.

"Ximena!"

Her dark eyes blinked back at him. "I must speak with you."

"Well, come in! How did you know where I live?"

She crooked her head at him momentarily and blinked again, then answered, "I have told you that I know many things." She pointed to the center of her chest. "I know them here."

He led her to the living room as Prewash kept her distance, slinking along the wall.

Mule stood and fixed his gaze on her piercing dark eyes.

"I take it you are Ximena," he said. "I'm Mule Hollis."

"Yes, I am Ximena." She turned to Lance then refocused on Mule again. "He is your friend?"

"Yes, he's my friend and he lives here."

"I can go back to my office if you two want to be alone," Mule said.

Ximena continued to stare into Mule's eyes. "No, please stay." She turned to Lance. "He needs to hear what I have to say as well as you."

They all sat on the couch and she again turned to Mule. "You have a green stone like the one I gave Lance."

Mule was a bit taken aback by the statement and looked over at Lance. "Did you tell her about that?"

"Nope," he said, then turned to Ximena. "How did you know about that?"

She smiled. "As I said, I know *many* things." She turned back to Mule. "May I see it?"

He was obviously confused by this unexpected conversation, but he stood. "Sure, it's in my office," and he left to retrieve it.

"I like him, he is a good man...a truly good man."

"Yes, he is."

Mule returned and handed the stone to her. She clenched it in her fist, held it to her heart, and closed her eyes. Beads of sweat formed on her forehead, then she reached out with her other hand and pulled Mule's hand close to her fist. "Take it and close your hand," she said.

Mule did as he was instructed, then she grasped both of his wrists and her eyes rolled back. He felt an intense burning where her hands touched him. He felt his face flush.

She released his hands and took a deep breath.

"This stone was no accident," she said. "And now your stone and Lance's stone are joined through me."

He relaxed his grip on the stone. "I'm not sure I understand. It's just a keepsake."

"It will protect you...*they* will help protect both of you and when you both have your stones and are together, their power will grow."

"Is there anything else we need to know about this?" Lance asked.

She shook her head. "I must go now," she said as she stood.

Lance followed her to the door and as they walked, he detected an aroma of incense on her clothes. She turned to him after he opened the door.

"I know you have feelings for me."

"Yes, you know many things." He smiled and she giggled.

Sam had said he thought she was eighteen but she looked much older. She was short, about five-foot-two and her eyes seemed to glisten up at him as they reflected in the bright moonlight.

"I have feelings for you as well, but...we must not act on them. I have work to do and you face great danger. I dare not allow my focus to fade, for your sake." She took a deep breath. "I could not bear such a loss."

"What do you mean?"

"I am still new to this life. I watched my *tia abuela* do this work for many years but I still have much to learn. I must go now, but I have one more thing to tell you. The vision of a word I do not understand keeps coming into my head when I see you and Sam...and Mule, for he is part of this connection now. Penumbra...I do not know what it means, but I know we must all beware of the penumbra."

Lance's heart pounded. "I don't know what it means either."

"We will understand soon, I feel this." She rose on her tiptoes and kissed him on the cheek, then turned his head and briefly kissed his lips.

She returned to her station wagon and hurried it down the road as Lance stood transfixed.

Mule had been watching them from the couch. When Lance returned to the living room gently touching his cheek he said, "You got it bad, chum."

"It's more than that," Lance said. "She warned me about something called penumbra."

"What is that?"

"That librarian from New Mexico mentioned the same thing. I have no idea what it means, but it's all tied up with this mess and I'm going to find out everything I can about it. I'll tell you another thing, too...I'm heading back to New

Mexico." He looked Mule right in the eyes. "And you aren't stopping me this time, either."

He picked up the phone. "Sam? I want to borrow your pack and whatever other equipment I can, except maybe a sleeping bag and mess kit. I have those already."

"Can't we do that tomorrow?"

"Sorry, I need it tonight. I want to leave early tomorrow morning."

"Can we talk about it?"

"I need to get up there and check out something Ximena told me. She also told me to beware the penumbra."

"Yeah, I remember that word...the librarian mentioned it."

"It must have something to do with everything this Dave character is involved in."

"You sure you don't just have a touch of..."

"The fever? No, it's based on a feeling I got from Ximena. I'll be by in a few minutes."

"Okay, I'll pull out what I can grab. Most of my kit is together. It's a little dusty."

When Lance returned from Sam's house with the equipment, he began to pack.

"She told us our little charms were linked and were stronger if we were together," Mule reminded him.

"I don't care right now. You can't go hiking off into the back country...you're not in good enough shape."

"I'll grant you that, but I could run interference for you."

"You can do that here. Besides, I need you to watch the dog. I'm going and that's all there is to it. And I'll need to take another look at that note we found in Dave's truck."

"I don't understand the hurry, Lance."

"Hey, you did it your way, now I am doing it my way."

Mule disappeared into his office and returned holding the note.

"I remember most of it, just want to get another look at it."

"Just copy it down."

"Don't want to risk it being found if I'm ambushed like Dave." He stared intently at the paper for several seconds. "I can remember that, there really isn't much to it." He returned the note to Mule.

"All right, then, I guess I'll turn in and talk to you before you leave." Mule turned and went to his bedroom.

In the morning, Prewash pawed at Mule's door. He got up and peeked in Lance's room. The door was open and everything was neat and tidy, like it usually was, except Lance was not there. He took the dog to the front door and let her out. He could see that Lance's truck was not in the driveway.

"He said he was taking off and he did," he said to Prewash. "The boy's got no sense in him."

Thirteen

A regular customer entered the café a few days later and asked Smidgeon a curious question. "What's going on? There are people lined up at a station wagon outside."

"I don't know what you mean." Smidgeon momentarily looked to the side as Holly approached with a menu.

"There's a dusty station wagon out in the parking lot with three people standing beside it. Looks like they're talking to some girl."

"Holly, would you help this gentleman find a table? I need to go outside and check on something."

"Yes ma'am. Come this way, sir."

Smidgeon looked across the parking lot and blinked in amazement. The customer was right. Smidgeon approached the car and recognized Ximena sitting in the driver's seat. A young man was leaning through the window, speaking softly to her in Spanish. Two older women standing behind him moved back when they spotted Smidgeon coming. She saw Ximena pull something from her bag and hand it to the man, who thrust something into Ximena's lap before hurrying away. He glanced back at Smidgeon, as if he were embarrassed.

"Ximena! What are you doing?"

"People in need find me wherever I go," she said.

"What did you give him?" She approached and saw a wad of bills in Ximena's lap. "Or I guess I should ask, what did you sell him?"

"A love charm. He's trying to capture someone's heart."

The two old women giggled but stopped when Smidgeon turned and fixed her gaze on them.

"You can't be doing this out in my parking lot."

"I came to see Lance and Sam. As I said, these people," she waved at the old women, "find me wherever I go."

"What do they want?"

"I don't know until they talk to me. Usually it is love or revenge." Ximena said something to them in Spanish and waved the old women away. They quietly chattered as they slowly made their way to a nearby pickup.

"There is a small *parque* nearby. I will talk to them there."

"Lance isn't here."

"Why would he leave? I told him...there is danger!"

"Honey, danger has a way of finding Sam and Lance, whether you are around or not."

Ximena started her car. "I will be back after I deal with the two women."

Sam was waiting at the door when Smidgeon returned.

"What was that all about?"

"Oh that? Just *your* witch casting spells in my parking lot."

"What?"

126

"Well, she says these people find her wherever she goes. I watched her sell a love charm. Who knows what those ladies want. Most likely revenge on somebody. If so, they'll probably add me to the list. But she said she came to see you and Lance and I told her he was gone. She was pretty upset when she heard that."

"Still scratching my head over him leaving so suddenly, but he's a grown man."

"I'd prefer a little more notice," Smidgeon said. "But I guess he's owed a few breaks."

Holly approached them. "That was Lance's witch lady, wasn't it?"

"Oh, I think she's Sam's witch lady, too," Smidgeon countered.

~ * ~

Lance stood outside his truck in the Roswell police parking lot. He'd gone in and asked that Detective Michaels meet him outside.

"Oh, it's you," Michaels said. "I was expecting Mule Hollis again."

"Just me this trip."

"I guess Mule filled you in...I don't have anything new, if that's what you're after."

"Partially, but what I really want to know is how I go about hiking into the wilderness near Capitan. You have any suggestions?"

Michaels laughed. "I've done a little hiking out there, but not in a while. That's all part of a wilderness area managed by the forest service. Pretty big, too, thirty-five thousand acres."

"Are there trails?"

"There are a lot, including Jeep trails, but most of those are pretty rough. You need topo maps. You got any of those?"

"Not yet."

"Lance, it's the real deal out there. You can go in a short distance on some trails for a day hike, but if you are going deeper, you're going to need to be prepared."

"I've got most everything I need but the maps. Where's the forest service headquarters?"

"Ruidoso, I think."

"Then I'm heading there."

"Be careful."

"I'm not new to this."

"But you're new to this area. It might be tougher than you think."

"I'm sure I'll be okay. Thanks for the info."

"Good luck," Michaels said.

As he drove off, Lance looked back and could see Michaels shaking his head.

Before he left town, he noticed a small store that looked like it had hunting supplies, so on a hunch, he stopped and inquired about some maps.

"Topo maps? Sure, we've got a few. Where you headed?"

"Capitan Mountains."

The clerk left and returned with some folded papers. "I've got a couple of Forest Service maps."

Lance paid the man and returned to his truck. He checked them over and quickly spotted the Capitan and Sunset peaks on one of them. He concentrated his attention on the area to the south of the two mountains.

"That looks like my best bet as a starting point," he said and he revved the truck's engine.

~ * ~

Sam sat down just as Mule was chewing his last bite of *Huevos Rancheros Especial.*

Mule pushed the empty plate away from him. "That is some good eating."

Sam smiled and looked around, making sure Smidgeon wasn't listening and whispered, "It was my first love here."

"So, suffice it to say there has been no word from Lance. It's been three days."

"Nope, not a word."

"Dang it. I told him not to go without me."

"I'm not sure what he expects to find. Believe me, hiking alone is hard, I did it for years. And he's trying it in a new area with some real mountains. The little bumps north of here were tough, but from what I've heard it is nothing like they have out there."

"And what's he doing for food?"

"I gave him a few packets of freeze-dried food I had, along with some potted meat, enough for several days, but it's water he has to worry about. If he's been hiking all this time, I imagine he'll be worn out by now, so I'm sure we'll hear from him soon."

The door opened and they both turned their heads. Ximena stood at the threshold looking all around the dining room. She saw Mule and Sam and hurried over to them.

"Mister Mule, I feel a great danger for Lance. You must do something." She sat down heavily, clutching her large cloth bag to her chest.

"There isn't much I can do. We don't even know where he is." Mule leaned toward her and added, "He decided to do this after talking to you the other night."

"This is not what we discussed. I think he had this idea before."

Sam interrupted. "Ximena, it is a big area and we only have the tiniest idea of where he is."

She lowered her head. "You are right. Nothing can be done. We have to trust the power of his stone to protect him."

"He has a stone? Like mine?" Sam asked.

"*Si.* Different, but the same. Like his," she said, pointing at Mule.

Mule blushed. "Yeah," he said, "like mine. They're both adamite, at least that's what the guy said when I bought it."

"From Mexico," Ximena added.

Mule nodded. "It might help us if we knew what kind of danger you see."

"Something evil is following him. A dark force. That is all I know. If he talks to you, tell him he must return at once."

"We'll do the best we can," Sam said.

"Tell him, it is *my* wish."

"I will."

"I will, too," Mule added.

With that, Ximena rose and hurried out the door.

Smidgeon approached from the kitchen and asked, "What was that all about?"

"I think she feels the same way about Lance as he feels about her," Mule said.

Sam chimed in, "Except she feels it on a different plane from us normal folks."

"I don't know about that, but I do know this." Mule fished the stone out of his pocket. "When she was talking about the stones and about Lance being in danger, this thing got mighty warm. I could feel it right through my pocket."

"Really?" Sam picked up the stone. "It's a completely different type of stone from mine."

"Like I said, the guy I bought it from in Capitan told me it was called adamite."

"It's cool now. You sure it got warm?"

"Almost hot. She said our stones were linked somehow through her. I'm not sure I buy that. For that matter, I'm not sure I buy any of her hooey, but I'm telling you, it did, in fact, get warm."

"Did Lance say anything else before he left?"

"He mentioned something like penumbra."

"Yeah, he told me that. The librarian said the old padre who buried the cache also mentioned penumbra. I don't think it's anything one could find. Judging from the dictionary meaning, it's basically a shadow."

Mule examined the stone as he turned it with his fingers. "Hmmmm, seems like we're all just chasing a curtain of shadows."

~ * ~

Lance took a sip of water. "I should have listened to everybody and stayed home." He rested against a boulder as he surveyed the mountain peaks in front of him.

"Sam said something about the saddle being a dip between two peaks. That one," he said to himself pointing to the left, "must be Capitan and the other is Sunset."

He'd been hiking up a dry wash all day and it was rough going. He shook his canteen and calculated he had barely enough water to get back to his truck. He looked up and down the wash. "I could get closer if I had a jeep. Wonder if Loot's old jeep would make it up here?" he mused. He attached the canteen to his belt and sighed.

"I guess I should head back."

"*Bueno.*"

Lance spun around. "Who said that?"

He blinked crusted trail dust from his eyes as he scanned every direction. It had been barely a whisper, but he was certain he had heard it. His best guess was that it came from a line of boulders to the north of him. He squinted against the glaring sunlight but could see nothing. He took a deep breath and began to make his way south when he abruptly fell down a small incline, twisting his ankle slightly.

"I swear, it felt like somebody shoved at me," he muttered.

He dropped his pack and rubbed at the outside of his boot. He felt the small gun he always kept inside the boot as he did this. He stood and tested his ankle.

"Sore, but if I can take it even a little easy...whoa."

He reached into his watch pocket and fingered the little stone Ximena had given him. "How'd that danged thing get hot all of a sudden?" He pulled it out to look at it, but it was cool to the touch.

As he walked he continued talking to himself. "I need to be able to drive way up this jeep trail, or at least get an earlier start with more water. My gut tells me this is the right spot."

He made his way to a crude junction where two rough trails intersected. He turned west and relaxed a bit because he knew he'd parked a couple of miles down. He'd stopped when the path got too rough for his truck's aging suspension.

The truck was in a small turnout, just as he had left it. He managed to return the way he had come, slowly navigating the rough road. He took it slow and easy and knew he'd soon be on a better road. As he approached his next turn, he saw the trail was blocked by a car he recognized as a Mercury.

"Wha...?"

A man got out and stood facing him. Lance slowed and when he got closer he recognized the face.

"Earl," he murmured under his breath as he parked and got out of his truck.

As he approached the grinning figure, he thought to himself, "This is probably exactly what happened to Dave."

Fourteen

"Well, well, well, look who I found. I recognized the truck back down the road...I knew I'd seen it at that café in Texas where I tracked down Holly. I followed you until you turned up that trail, but I knew your heap couldn't make it too far up that way, so's I figured you'd be back before too long. I guess you're working with *her* on this?"

"I don't know what you mean."

"Come on now. Why else would you be out here? You've got to be looking for the same thing we're looking for."

"We?"

"Ding, get out here. I want you to drive that truck."

A short, stocky man with a scar down the left side of his face and a shock of blond hair got out and stood next to Earl.

"Is it a stick?"

"Well," Earl said to Lance. "Is it?"

"Yeah, it's a stick."

"Can't drive no stick, Earl."

"Then you drive the Merc, and our friend here will drive the truck. Guess I'm riding with you in the truck, cowboy."

"To where?"

Earl laughed as he motioned with his gun. "Never you mind."

~ * ~

The evening rush was over and Sam was busy refilling table condiments in the dining room. He looked up and was surprised to see Holly come into the café.

"Did you forget something?"

"I had a message to call Earl so I did. He said he'd kill me if I don't give him what he wants." She sat near Sam and cried. "I don't even know what it is he wants."

"We'll figure this out, okay?"

"How did he find out where I was staying?"

"He probably called around until he found you."

"Maybe it would be better for everyone if I just left. I'm obviously not safe here."

"That doesn't bring us any closer to finding Dave, does it?"

"Nothing you guys have done has helped. Have you heard from Lance?"

"No, and I'm a bit worried that we haven't."

"Why did he go off alone? He should have taken Mule with him."

As she said this, the phone rang and Sam limped over to answer it. "Hello, Mossback."

He talked in low tones and faced away from Holly because she was watching him intently from across the room. Sam looked grim as he hung up and turned around.

"Was that Lance?"

"Yeah, but only briefly. In the movies, they'd call it providing proof of life, I guess. He only got out a couple of words before Earl grabbed the phone."

Holly gasped. "Earl? What did he say?"

"Basically a repeat of what he said to you. They want me to deliver you and the note by tomorrow evening or we will both die, along with Lance and Dave. He said, and I quote, they'd track down the café owner and kill her, too. All they want is you and the note."

"Note? He told me the same thing over the phone. What is he talking about...that stupid paper Lance and Mule found?"

"Yeah, it was hidden in Dave's truck and now we know why he put it away. He wasn't supposed to have it."

"Why didn't we just give it to Earl when he was here? Then Dave would already be back with us."

"I doubt that," Sam said in a stern tone.

"Why?"

"People like this keep their secrets close. If Dave is alive, he's only good to them as long as they need him to get what they want. Once they get that, they don't need him anymore. I'd say Lance is in the same boat."

Tears began to stream down her face. "How can you be so sure?"

"Once they get the note, both Dave and Lance become liabilities. Right now, Earl is using them as an incentive."

"But why do they want me?"

"Good question. The truth is...I don't know. It's probably because they need something else from Dave that isn't in the note."

"So what do we do now? Do you have the note?"

"Mule's got it or, rather, I hope he still has it."

"Why would you say that?"

"I'm hoping Lance didn't take it with him."

"If he had, they wouldn't have asked for it."

"Lance isn't stupid, but he is stubborn. He wouldn't have given it to them."

Sam returned to the phone and called Mule's number.

"Mule, this is Sam."

"Have you heard from Lance?"

"Yes. Earl has him. He wants the note. Oh, and he wants Holly, too."

"Well, I have the note and we already know what it says, so I've got no problem giving it to him. Is Lance okay?"

"Yeah, so far. They yanked the phone from him before he got more than a couple of words out."

"What else did Earl say?"

"He wants to meet in New Mexico. He'll call later with a time and a place."

"I figure if he wants Holly, too, he's looking to tie up loose ends. The more people involved, the more loose ends."

"In other words, everybody is at risk. Listen, Holly is here with me; he tried to call her at the motel first. She came here after he threatened to kill her."

"Okay, is Smidgeon there?"

"No, she's at the house."

"You call Smidgeon and have her come down there and I'll meet you all in a few minutes."

"Okay."

Sam phoned Smidgeon, then returned to Holly.

"We're all meeting here in a few minutes. Don't worry...we'll come up with some kind of plan."

"I take the note with me and go meet Earl, that's the plan."

"We'll talk about it when everybody gets here." Sam flipped the closed sign in the door then called out to the kitchen. "Chuy! We're closing early, like now."

Chuy stuck his head out the door. "Okay, boss. I've got everything almost ready anyway."

Sam appreciated the fact that Chuy was content to just get his work done and mind his own business.

Mule and Smidgeon arrived just after Chuy left.

"What the heck is going on, Sam?" Smidgeon asked. Sam filled her in. She wrinkled her brow and looked at all of them in turn. "So we need to come up with a plan of action."

"Well, we can't leave Lance with that goon," Sam said.

"Goons," Mule corrected. "Earl has a partner, a guy named Ding, according to the detective in Roswell. But the note is the only bargaining chip we have. If we let that go, Lance is likely done for."

"Dave, too," Holly said. "As far as bargaining chips go, we have two because apparently Earl wants me, too. Maybe if I do what he wants, they'll at least let Lance go."

Mule shook his head. "People like this don't let witnesses go, Holly. I'm pretty sure it's the reason they want you, too. Still no mention of this Rey Mendoza either."

Sam slapped a palm on the table. "Anybody who goes is dead."

"Right." Mule's grave expression was mirrored in all of their faces. "Any plan we come up with has to be layered. I don't think they know about me, so that's a plus. Earl has seen you two," he said, pointing at Sam and Smidgeon and moved his finger toward Holly, "and of course he knows you."

"So, Mule, you're our wild card," Sam said.

"Exactly."

Holly's eyes began to tear. "I hope you aren't going to leave me here alone."

"Not at all," Mule said. "I think I may have a plan, but if things go wrong, they'll do whatever they can to get to you."

"You really think they'd kill me?" Holly asked.

Smidgeon reached out and touched Holly's arm. "Honey, all of us *will* be killed if we don't turn the tables on them somehow."

Mule and Sam nodded in agreement. They were all startled when the phone rang again. Smidgeon rose to answer it, but Sam held up his hand.

"Let me get it," he said.

He limped to the counter and spoke quietly, writing something on an order pad while he talked. He returned to the group and read them what he had written.

"Dusk tomorrow at the parking lot for the Lincoln Historic Site. I'm supposed to be there with Holly." He turned to Smidgeon. "Along with that woman with the long, dark hair."

"Loose ends," Mule muttered, adding, "I've passed through Lincoln the last couple of times I went to Capitan. It's a tiny place, but I remember seeing that little historical park. Ain't much life in that town outside of tourist season, but it must mean they're holed up nearby."

"We go in two cars, Mule's and somebody else's."

"Mine," Holly said. "They'll probably expect it. Should we contact the police, too?"

Mule said, "Well, I guess we could...but only if we want everybody to die."

Holly gasped. "You really think so?"

"Too many cooks. The only way we have a hope of getting Lance back..."

"And Dave," Holly added.

"Yes, and Dave, is to surprise them."

Mule went out to his car and returned with a map. They all studied the locations and he pointed to Arabela where they had found Dave's truck, then to Capitan, where they had talked to Mitch Blalock. "Lincoln is convenient to both locations, so it's not a big surprise they want to meet there. I'm sure it's got to be close to where they're hiding."

"So what's the plan?" Sam asked.

"I go to Lincoln first and scout it, you guys head out a while later and we rendezvous in Roswell. By then I'll know how we can set these goons up. I'll return to Lincoln ahead of you, hide, and be ready to jump in when they show up."

"Still a lot of holes," Sam said.

"Yes, but I can't even begin to fill them in until I get there and see the layout," Mule said. He turned to Smidgeon. "You still got that forty-five?"

She patted her purse, "Right here."

"I've got a can of mace," Holly added. "I always carry it around."

"You might get a chance to use it," Sam said.

~ * ~

Mule arrived in Lincoln about noon the next day. There was not much to see except for a few houses, a couple of stores, a small Catholic church, and, of course, the historic site. Mule parked and paid his fee before he walked around the grounds.

"We close at five," the attendant told him.

There were a number of buildings on the property, and while he walked around, he considered the situation they all faced. If they met in the parking lot, they would all be obscured somewhat from the road.

"That's got to be what they want," he mumbled to himself.

He scouted the buildings and decided he'd be able to hide behind any one of them, but he'd need to park his car someplace else and walk over. He settled on the small church building across the street.

"They'd still see it," he mused, "but it's not unusual for someone to visit a church."

There was a small round tower near the road, part of the historic site. Mule thought he might be able to start by hiding behind it and make his way closer to get the drop on his prey.

Satisfied, he drove back to Roswell for the rendezvous with the others. Holly had suggested a small park and playground she was familiar with, and he found his way there and waited.

When Holly's car pulled next to his, he felt a wave of relief. Sam was driving.

"How did everything go?" Smidgeon asked as she got out of the passenger seat. Holly was asleep in the back.

Sam got out and told Mule, "She took a tranquilizer. She's been out almost the whole way."

"Lordy," Mule reached into the back seat and shook her. "Miss Holly? You need to wake up."

She sleepily opened her eyes and looked around. "Oh, we're there. Okay. Give me a minute, I'm woozy. I'm sorry, but I was just so upset."

"So," Sam said, "what did you find?"

"Ain't much cover, but I think I can make do." He stooped down and drew a crude diagram of the site in the dirt. "This is the layout of the parking lot. It'd be better if we could get them over to this corner," he said, pointing. "It's blocked from the road by one of the buildings. These other buildings on the site provide vantage points. I can park at a church across the street and hide."

"What time does the park close?"

"Five. I doubt we'd draw much attention after it's closed, and even if the police were called, it would be a while before they could respond. I imagine Earl knows this, too, or he wouldn't have suggested this place."

"You're probably right there. I think he expects a quick transaction."

Mule handed Sam the paper. "He'll expect you to have this."

"Did you copy it?"

"Of course I did," Mule laughed.

"Silly they didn't think of that," Smidgeon said.

Sam read the note again. "It's strange, why insist on this piece of paper?"

"Unless..." Smidgeon said, "there is something else about this note." She took it and examined it closely. She held it up to the sun and squinted. "There's more!"

"What do you mean?" Mule asked.

"Invisible ink. We used to do this when I was a kid. I can see the outline of something but the sun is too bright. We need a candle."

"We don't have time...maybe the interior light in the car?" Sam suggested.

Smidgeon got in the car and held the note in front of the light. "It's a map, with an outline and one word."

"What's the word?" Sam asked.

"Penumbra."

He took the note and verified. "Yep, that's what it says. Somebody give me a piece of paper and a pen."

Smidgeon pulled the requested items out of her purse and Sam glanced back and forth at the note while he drew a crude half-circle of irregular shapes, with an arrow pointing to the upper right. Then there was another image, with Penumbra written under it.

Sam squinted at the image. "I don't know what that is, a bird? Those look like wings."

Smidgeon took a turn and said, "For the life of me, I think it looks like an angel."

"What did Dave get us all into?" Holly asked.

Mule remarked, "I don't know, but it's time to go. Give me about a twenty minute head start. I'll park at the church. There ain't much else there, so the place will be easy for you to spot."

Sam said, "Got it. Be careful."

"I always am," Mule said.

Inwardly, he didn't feel quite as confident. He had an uneasy feeling as he drove away.

He mumbled to himself, "A lot of things could go wrong."

Fifteen

Smidgeon and Holly walked toward the car, but Sam turned and said, "I'm going to hit the bathroom before we leave. Anybody else? Who knows when we'll get another chance down the road."

The women both shook their heads as they got in the car.

"Just hurry it up," Smidgeon said.

Sam had the small building to himself, but as he washed his hands, a faint voice startled him.

"Looks like a big mess of trouble."

"Loot! Would you stop popping up like that?"

"I can't help it, I mean, according to my peculiar condition and all."

"Okay, I guess you can't. What's up, do you know anything?"

"I've been following along but I can't say I quite understand it all."

"Lance is missing and we're going to see if we can rescue him."

"I don't know about that, but I can tell you this...something dark is behind all of this, Sam. I can't quite see it, but I know it ain't good."

"A bunch of thieving treasure hunters are behind it."

"This may be more than that. I'll help if I can."

"What can you do?"

"I've helped you more than you know."

"You have?"

"Yep. Trust me, I'll be around."

With that, Loot faded.

Sam's heart was pounding and beads of sweat had formed on his forehead. He splashed water on his face and dried it with paper towels. Back at the car, Smidgeon was obviously agitated.

"Dang, thought maybe I was going to have to barge in there to check on you."

"Sorry." He looked back at Holly and asked, "She's asleep again?"

Smidgeon sighed. "Can't believe that girl. Still, she's suffered a heap of misery these last few weeks."

"Yeah, let her sleep. We'd best be on our way," Sam said, and they continued down the road.

~ * ~

Mule parked his Olds and checked his watch. It was late afternoon and he looked toward the sun. "I'd say it's about a half hour from setting." He glanced down the highway. "Hopefully they should be along any minute."

He anxiously pulled the thirty-eight from his shoulder holster and checked it before returning it to its resting place. He smoothed the coat around it then reached into a side pocket and felt for the rounds of loose ammunition he had hastily stashed. "Should be plenty...more in the glove box if I need it," he murmured.

The highway was clear of traffic, so he made his way across to the far side of the small tower and crouched down.

"The building over there would be better, *señor*."

Mule spun around in a state of shock.

"Ximena?"

"*Sí.*"

"How did you get here? How did you know?"

"I see many things...you *know* this. Our friends will be here soon. So will Lance. Until then, we must wait."

"Yes, but..."

"It is simple, Mister Mule. The stones, they talk to me. Now we must move. *They* will be here soon and they must not see us."

Mule and Ximena found a protected spot behind a bush next to one of the buildings and crouched down. In a few minutes, they heard a car pull into the small lot and park. He peeked around the corner and verified it was Holly's car. "I see Sam, Smidgeon, and Holly."

"There is also another," Ximena added. "Sam's protector is with him."

Mule looked again and counted. "I only see three."

Ximena showed a demure smile. "Oh, you cannot see this one, but he is there."

Mule didn't have time to dwell on her cryptic comment because he heard another vehicle.

"Wait," he whispered, "there are two of them! What the..."

He recognized one as Lance's truck. The other was a Mercury sedan.

"That's who we're waiting for," Mule whispered.

"I know. Lance is with them."

"Yeah, they have him driving his own truck. He probably has a gun on him."

Ximena began fumbling in her bag and pulled out a crystal of some sort.

"What are you doing?"

"Never mind. You do what you are here to do. I will do what *I* am here to do."

Mule continued observing as he carefully pulled his pistol.

~ * ~

Sam took a deep breath as he heard two vehicles pull into the parking lot. "Smidgeon, you stay low with your gun. They're only expecting me and Holly."

She opened the door a crack. "I'll be ready to jump out."

Holly was shivering. "Sam, I'm scared. You have the paper, right?"

"I do. And we've copied it all down, even the hidden stuff, so we don't need it anymore."

He got out of the car and Holly followed. They stood together along the rear fender of her car.

One man exited the Mercury. Sam didn't recognize him, so he assumed he was looking at the guy Mule called Ding. He was armed with a handgun.

"Hey, Holly."

"Ding, you lowlife, where's Dave?"

"We'll take care of everything as soon as we get that note he stole from us."

"What's that supposed to mean?"

Earl exited the truck and kept his gun pointed at Lance as he slowly got out.

Lance cried out, "Don't give them nothing, Sam!"

Earl gestured with his gun. "Shut up, you."

Sam held up his hands. "No need for the hardware, we're unarmed."

"You don't understand the stakes, mister," Ding said.

"Oh, I think I do. I've read all about the Archangel Cache. Listen, I've been a treasure hunter for a long time and I know it is always one dead end after another. This story's been around for almost three hundred years...don't you think somebody must have found it by now?"

"Never mind, I don't care what you think about it. You're Sam, right?"

He nodded. "We just want our friend. I have the note we found in Dave's truck. It's simple...you give us Lance and Dave, I give you the note."

"We need Dave and Holly even after we get the note."

Earl turned toward the Mercury. "Shut up, Ding."

"That wasn't the deal. Listen, I'll wad it up and swallow it."

"Then we'll kill Dave, your friend, and of course, you, and after that we'll cut it out of you."

Holly said, "Give me the note, Sam. I'll go with them."

Sam put a hand on her shoulder. "That's not going to be part of the deal, Holly."

Suddenly there was a small figure standing among all of them.

Lance yelled, "Ximena!"

Sam whispered, "Where did *she* come from?"

Holly responded, "I don't know, Sam, suddenly she was just...there."

Ximena approached Earl, her left fist clenched at her side. She pointed with her right index finger.

"Release him!"

Ding kept switching his aim between Ximena and Sam while Earl pulled Lance closer and placed the gun barrel firmly against the back of his head.

"Why don't you just go away, little lady? Ain't nothing you can do here," Earl said before yelping in pain and dropping his gun. As he reached down for it, Lance bolted to the other side of his truck and crouched down for a moment. When he stood again he was holding his own gun.

"I don't know where you went to crime school, but when you take a guy prisoner, you really ought to frisk him."

Mule came running around the side of the building with his gun drawn.

Earl reached down to retrieve his gun but dropped it again. "Ahhhh, it's red hot! How're you doing that?"

Ximena, silent, glared at him, still pointing.

Smidgeon jumped out of the back seat with her forty-five trained on Ding. "Drop it!"

Ding took a second to consider his situation, then lowered his gun and ran to the Mercury. Earl followed, barely getting into the passenger seat as Ding hit the gas and the car sprayed gravel as they made their escape.

"Aw," Sam said, holding out and waving a small piece of paper. "They forgot their note."

Lance holstered his weapon. "They ain't the brightest bulbs in the pack."

"But they still have Dave," Holly said. She turned to Lance. "Is he okay?"

"To tell the truth, I never saw Dave the whole time." Then he realized Ximena was still standing in the same spot, as if in a trance. He ran over to her and shouted in her face. "Ximena? Ximena!"

She collapsed in his arms and he lowered her to the ground. She whispered, "I could not let them hurt you."

"How did she show up so suddenly?" Smidgeon asked.

Mule crouched and checked for a pulse. "She was hiding over there with me," he said, pointing. "Next thing I knew, she was in the middle of everything. Frankly, I don't remember her leaving my side. Suddenly she was in a face-off with Earl.

"My bag, I need my bag," Ximena whispered.

Mule looked up. "She must have left her bag back where we were hiding. I'll go get it."

Lance cradled her head in his hands. "She's flushed. Does anybody have some water?"

"I do," Holly said and she ran to the car.

"I am fine; give me a moment to recover my strength." Her hand was still clenched and she motioned it to Lance. "Take my crystal. Be careful with it, it holds great power."

Lance cupped the stone in his hands and Mule returned with Ximena's bag.

"There is a handkerchief in the bag. Wrap it tightly around the crystal and place it back inside," she said. She took a deep breath and sat up. "I...am...feeling better," she stammered, still out of breath.

Mule retrieved Earl's gun and closely examined it. "The dang thing is wrecked. Can't get the clip out or anything."

"At least we got Lance back," Smidgeon said.

"But we still don't know where Dave is," Holly said, sobbing.

"Like I said, I never saw him."

Mule interrupted the conversation. "I think we need to get out of here. Lance, are your keys still in the truck?"

"Yeah."

"Ximena, where is your car?"

"By the road that way," she said, pointing.

"I'm parked at the church across the street. Sam, I think you should drive Ximena in her car. I'll take you down to get it. Holly, can you drive your car?"

Smidgeon took a look at the tears streaming down Holly's cheeks. "I think I had better drive Holly's car."

"Okay, then, let's get out of here. We've got a lot of miles to cover," Mule said and they all took off back to Texas.

~ * ~

The station wagon was old and seemed to shake at certain speeds, so Sam was driving at just under the limit. He tried to keep up with Mule but gradually fell behind the newer Oldsmobile.

"Thank you," Ximena said. "I am feeling better, but I have never used that before. My crystal has great power but it wearied me. I need to always remember I am a just a novice."

"What did you do back there? That *was* you, right?"

"A powerful spell. There was some risk, but I feared he would harm Lance and I could not let anything happen to him."

Sam glanced at Ximena and could see she was shivering.

"You like him? Like boyfriend, girlfriend like?"

"I have never been allowed time for such things. My *tia abuela* Asminda required I stay with her and learn."

"*Tia abuela*, what is that?" Sam asked; his meager Spanish not providing an answer.

"She was the sister of my...*abuela*. I think the English word is grandmother."

"Oh, so Asminda was your great-aunt."

"*Si*. She was very old when she first met you, but her powers were great. When I was very young, she made the decision to give me..."

"The power to do such things?"

"*Si*. May I ask you something? Does Lance have a woman in his life?"

"He's pretty shy around women. I know he's been out with a few, like on dates, but no one serious."

Ximena smiled. "That is good."

"So you, you think you two will maybe get together?"

She blushed. "I don't know."

"I thought you knew things."

"I do, but affairs of the heart are another matter."

"Don't you help people with things like love potions and charms?"

"Other people, *señor*. Of course, it is possible for me to do such things for myself but it is not right. If it is to be, for me, it must be without such help. *Tía* Asminda never married, and cautioned me to be very careful in such matters."

"But you like him."

"Oh, yes. This is why I could not let them hurt him."

"And you used your powers to follow us and find him."

"I had given him a stone bound to me, joined to my protection."

"Like the protection Asminda gave to me."

"Yes. Mr. Mule also has such a stone."

Suddenly, Ximena's face went blank and she stared straight ahead.

"What's wrong? Are you okay?"

She nodded weakly but said nothing.

"What is it?"

Ximena held up her hand and Sam kept quiet until Ximena finally turned to him.

"There is a spirit. An evil one. It spoke to me."

"Just now?"

She nodded. "Again...I am warned of the penumbra and all of you are in peril if you do not heed this warning."

"We keep hearing that word. What does it mean?"

"I do not know." She closed her eyes. "I am very tired."

"You've had a long day," Sam said, "go ahead and sleep."

As he drove south, Sam stared at the road and softly mumbled to himself, "Penumbra again, what the heck does it mean?"

Sixteen

Smidgeon, Lance, and Mule waited for Sam in the closed dining room after they had dropped Holly at the motel.

"Poor Holly," Smidgeon said.

Lance asked, "Do you think we should have left her alone over there?"

"We couldn't bring her here because she had taken something that made her really sleepy. I imagine she'll be okay. I think she's worn out by the worry. It's been an ongoing hell for her, but at least those guys didn't get what they were after."

"We don't know where that note came from, but surely someone copied it," Mule said.

"If so, why'd they want the note?" Smidgeon asked. "I mean, it stands to reason they must know about the invisible ink. If that's true, you'd think they would have written that down, too."

"Schoolboy stuff," he said. "Schoolboys love their secret codes."

Lance was busy wiping tables as they talked.

"Lance, what on earth are you doing?" Smidgeon asked.

"Just anxious. Keeping busy helps." He stopped and looked up. "There is one thing about keeping secrets...you don't write them down any more than necessary because that increases the chances of your secret getting out."

Mule tapped the table with his fingers. "I'll grant you that. And we didn't even consider a hidden message when we first found it."

"Yeah, and even though I memorized it, now it looks like I made a big mistake. I sure didn't know about that part," Lance added. "They obviously anticipated one of us going up there and that's how they grabbed me. I was a fool to go up there alone."

"Hah!" Mule laughed. "Glad you finally admit it."

Lance stopped his work and looked out the window. "Where are Sam and Ximena?"

"That old wagon," Mule said. "I wouldn't be surprised if they broke down."

"Sam would have called."

"If he could, but as you know, phones are few and far between out there. It's not like he could just whip one out of his pocket and call us."

"No, of course not. That's never going to happen," Smidgeon said. "But surely if they broke down, they'd get help sooner or later. I know he would manage to get someplace where he could call."

The phone rang. Smidgeon ran to the register area to answer it.

"Right on cue," Mule joked, "Probably him now."

"Or somebody fussing about us not being open," Lance said.

~ * ~

"Smidgeon? It's Sam."

"Where the heck are you? We've been back for a couple of hours!"

"We stopped to eat. I think we're in Artesia."

"How long does it take you two to eat?"

"It's Ximena. We stopped at a cafe here...she directed me to it. I went inside to get some food to take with us, and when I came back, a line had formed at her window. It's like people sense her presence and descend on her."

"That's crazy. Just like in our parking lot."

"Yeah. But she's almost done. I've fussed at her a couple of times, but I don't want to push her too hard."

"Why not? You've got to get back."

"I'm just a little afraid of her."

"You may have a point there. Look, we've been here waiting for you, but I'm beat. I think I'll just head on home and wait for you there."

"Sure, honey."

Smidgeon returned to the group. "It was Sam."

"They're okay?" Lance asked.

"Yeah. They stopped someplace to eat and she attracted a crowd."

"Oh, you mean..."

Smidgeon glared at Lance as she answered for him. "Yes. Peddling her witch work."

"You have to admit..."

"Stop, I don't even want to think about that...it makes my skin crawl."

"It was certainly a strange thing," Mule said. "In all my years in law enforcement I have never seen a gun in that condition. It was like all the parts inside were welded tight. I tossed the thing into a stock tank I spotted along the way here."

"Good riddance. Well, there's no need for us to hang around; they'll be hours. Remember, I've still got a business to run and we've got to open in the morning, so I'm heading home."

~ * ~

At the house, Smidgeon busied herself with housework. She always cleaned when she was anxious.

"Lance is the same way," she said to herself, as she remembered mildly fussing at him for wiping clean tables at the café.

Her thoughts were interrupted by the phone.

"It's Holly. Earl just called me and put Dave on the phone."

"What? He's okay?"

"He told me he was with Earl and Ding, and he begged me to bring the paper to them. Alone. Otherwise, they're going to kill him."

"Oh, dear. You're not going to do it, are you?"

"He said I don't have any other choice."

"Listen, if a man gives you just one choice, you have to figure out the other options he doesn't want you to think about. Either that or you need to consider possibilities he hasn't thought of yet. Where was he calling from?"

"He said they were near Carlsbad...they want to meet me in the parking lot of a store on the west side of town, on Lea Street. I need to be there at five tomorrow morning with that paper."

"Carlsbad ain't too far, but Sam has the paper and he's still not here."

Holly's voice trembled. "Oh, dear."

"Anyway, you shouldn't go there alone. Let me see if I can talk to Lance or Mule so we can figure something out."

Holly sobbed lightly. "Okay."

After hanging up, she started looking for Mule's number, but the phone rang again.

"Smidgeon?"

"Sam! Where are you?"

"We just pulled into Carlsbad. Ximena made me stop and call you."

Smidgeon's heart skipped a beat. "What?"

"She suddenly pointed at a pay phone on the side of the road and said I needed to call you right away. Is there anything wrong?"

"I *just* got off the phone with Holly. She told me Earl called and let her talk to Dave. *He's* in Carlsbad with Earl and Ding. She is supposed to go by herself along with the paper and meet them at a small store on Lea Street at five in the morning. She said it's on the west side of town."

"I have the paper."

"I know that. I was just fixing to call Mule to ask him what we should do when you called."

"Call Holly and tell her to stay put. I'll handle it."

"Sam, how can you face off with Earl and Ding? You don't even have a gun."

"I have Ximena."

"Oh, right, *Ximena.* So what are you going to do?"

"We'll probably just find a quiet place to sit and wait it out."

"How did she know you needed to call me?"

"I've learned to quit asking stuff like that. I'm not sure I want to know the answer."

"Yeah, I guess I can understand that. Keep in touch."

"I'll try. It's sometimes hard to find a pay phone."

"I know. I love you! Be careful."

"I always am. I love you, too."

Smidgeon hung up and called Holly at the motel.

"Sam is in Carlsbad!"

"Really? When is he coming back? I need that paper."

"He's going to meet them and try to get Dave."

"They said for *me* to come."

"Holly, he already has the paper and he's already there. And besides, he's not alone...he's still got Ximena with him."

"But they won't give him Dave, and after what she did last time, she'll probably just scare them away."

"I doubt they'd hand Dave over to you anyway. It sounds funny, but I think what they really want is you. Is there something else you haven't told us?"

"I'm not sure what you mean."

"Why are they so intent on you being involved?"

"Honestly, I don't know."

"Well, just sit tight. Please. Sam has what they say they want and he's already there."

"Since he has the paper, I guess I have no choice. Well, maybe I could just go up there and get it from him."

"Please don't do that. Sam is taking a big enough risk already. I think you'd endanger both your lives."

"Maybe you're right. What about Ximena, do you think she's in danger, too?"

"I think she can take care of herself."

~ * ~

"We wait?" Ximena asked.

"Yes. The men who took Lance want a meeting for this," Sam held out a paper.

"They want the one you call Holly as well."

Sam was no longer surprised by Ximena's insight. "Yes, but they aren't getting her this time out. We will meet them down the road at five in the morning."

"This paper has evil attached to it. I can feel it."

157

"I don't doubt that. No good can come from it, which is why I am willing to give it to them."

"What do you want from me?"

He grinned and said, "Just be yourself." He knew in his heart that she would do whatever she felt she needed to do.

"I cannot be anything else." She leaned to his shoulder. "We should rest now. Sleep."

~ * ~

Sam's eyes popped open. The last thing he remembered was one word, sleep. He looked at his watch and saw it was four-thirty. "How does she do that?" he mused under his breath.

"You would not understand."

"Oh, you're awake, too."

"I sleep lightly. I think we need to go to the meeting place."

Sam sat up. "You're right." He rubbed his face with his hands, trying to wipe away the sleep and started the car.

He found Lea Street and drove until he found the small store next to an even smaller drive-in; both were closed. He parked and glanced at his watch again. "Fifteen minutes."

At five, Sam saw a large sedan pull into the parking lot. He told Ximena to stay down. "They are only expecting one person...Holly."

She fumbled in her bag. "I will be ready."

Two figures exited the sedan and stood by the rear fender. Sam got out and faced them.

"You ain't Holly," Earl said.

"You're right, I'm not, but I was already in Carlsbad. I still have the paper you wanted to get in Lincoln."

Earl looked down at Ding then turned back to Sam. "We need Holly, too."

"Why?"

"I can't rightly say."

"Do you want the paper or not? I can just get right back in my car and leave."

Ding raised his hand. "We'll take the paper."

"Where's Dave?"

"Why do you want Dave?"

"Holly wants him."

"Then she should have come."

Sam took a deep breath. "I guess we have nothing more to discuss," he said as he turned back toward the car door.

"Wait," Ding said. "The paper."

"Why should I give it to you now?"

"Because we'll kill you and take it anyway."

Sam felt a burning along the front side of his hip and he knew it was the stone he carried in the watch pocket of his jeans. Suddenly, Ximena was standing among the three of them, glaring at the two men.

"You will kill no one," she said, clenching her fist.

Earl had been reaching behind his back, but he retracted his bandaged hand.

"The man in the trunk, give him to us, and we will give you the paper you want."

"That ain't the deal, lady."

"This *is* the deal. Give him to us."

"Maybe we should do it." Ding's voice was wavering. "He's no good to us, not really."

Earl wiped sweat from his forehead and pulled out his keys as he backed to the rear of the sedan and opened the trunk.

"Looks like this is your lucky day, Dave."

He pulled the bound and gagged figure out and led him to a space between Ximena and their sedan. Sam came forward, holding out the piece of paper. Earl shoved Dave to

Sam and grabbed the piece of paper. He rejoined Ding, pulled out a lighter and held it behind the paper and examined it.

"Yep, it's the real thing. You didn't know about this little detail."

Sam laughed. "Are you kidding?"

Earl seemed startled. "Well, you don't know the rest of it, so it won't do you any good."

"You have what you want, just leave us all alone."

"We'll see," Earl said. He and Ding returned to their car and raced off.

Sam untied Dave's bindings.

"Who are you guys?"

"Holly's a friend and she sent us, but we need to get out of here."

"Where we going? Back to Roswell?"

"No, we're heading south."

"Where?"

"To *Tejas*," Ximena said.

~ * ~

It was a busy morning at the café, and they were short-handed. During the lull between morning and noon customers, the phone rang, but it was not a takeout order.

"Smidgeon?" The voice was familiar. "This is Bea."

"Oh, hi. I didn't expect you to call. I thought it was another order."

"If it's too busy, I can call back."

"No, you caught me at a good time. What's up?"

"I found more information about the Archangel Cache."

"Really? Sam isn't here but I'll tell him. What is it?"

"I found out more about that gentleman Lance mentioned, Rey Mendoza. He is a direct descendent of Diego Mendoza. It turns out Diego is his great-great-great grandfather. Rey Mendoza lives in New Mexico, not far from Carlsbad and has a lot of criminal involvement. In the past, he was known to search for the treasure, and I suspect he may have some additional information about it that is missing from other accounts."

"Like what?"

"It's just a hunch...I really have no idea. Oh, and one other thing. Although Rey Mendoza never married, he apparently had one illegitimate child, a girl, with a woman named Patrice Blanca. The little girl was given up for adoption."

"What does that have to do with the treasure?"

"I don't know. I'm just reporting what I found. There's something else. Rey Mendoza is in a wheelchair. He lost the use of his legs several years ago in a car crash."

"That is a lot of stuff."

"There's more...I also researched known eclipses. A lunar eclipse did indeed occur on September 30, 1773, the day after the Feast of St. Michael."

"Why is that significant?"

"Well, for one thing, it verifies part of the story and helps it make more sense. They buried the stolen loot, then planned to make their escape during the eclipse. Something unusual must have happened during the eclipse."

"I guess I don't understand."

"Me either, but the word penumbra keeps coming up, and that word is commonly used during the phases of a lunar eclipse. I'm just passing along what I've found.

"Wow, you've been busy. Okay, I'll report all of this back to the others. Maybe they can make some sense out of it."

"I'll keep researching when I can. This is fun for me."

"I'm glad you're enjoying yourself. We aren't."

"What's wrong?"

"This whole thing has been messed up from the start. We all went on a wild goose chase to the middle of New Mexico yesterday and almost got ourselves killed. All over this silly treasure."

"Oh, I'm sorry. You want me to give it up?"

"No, no, we're in this too deep now, and I'm sure this is all helpful. I just don't know how it helps yet."

"You tell everyone to be careful, Smidgeon, okay? I like you guys."

"Thanks. We like you, too. I appreciate whatever help you can provide. I really do."

Smidgeon put the phone down and muttered under her breath, "Patrice Blanca."

Holly had just walked by with the coffee decanter in her hand when she stopped and dropped it. Glass and coffee exploded across the floor.

"Holly, what happened?"

She spun and said, "Did you say Patrice Blanca?"

"Yes. It was just something Bea told me on the phone."

"That...that's the name of my birth mother," Holly said. "My adoptive parents told me."

Smidgeon pointed to a table. "Sit down, honey, I think we need to have a little talk."

Seventeen

"I'm Sam," he said as they sped south. "This is Ximena."

"Name's Dave. How'd you know I was in the trunk?"

"We know all about you, Dave. Holly came to us for help and we've been on your trail for weeks."

"We? Who do you mean?"

"You'll meet everyone soon...there's a whole bunch of us."

"Well, the farther away from those two I can get, the better. I thought they were my buddies. Some friends they turned out to be. First they kidnapped me and then they held me prisoner for weeks." Dave chuckled. "Of course I did steal that treasure note from them, so maybe I brought it on myself. How'd you get it?"

"Some friends of mine found the note in your truck along with your gun."

"Out in Arabela where I broke down?"

"Capitan, where the police had it towed. The gun was handed over to the police."

"Oh, man, the cops are involved? And probably my parole officer, too. I'm screwed."

"The way things have been going, that may be the least of your problems. We can work out all the details later."

"It's all about a treasure, man. I still remember the details."

"We copied the note, even the hidden parts."

"Hidden parts?"

"Yeah. We can fill you in about everything once we get safely to Van Horn."

"Van Horn? You mean in Texas?"

"That's where we're headed."

"I'm not supposed to leave the state without permission."

"Like I said, we can help you deal with that later, but that's where we're headed."

~ * ~

"So, don't you worry about Sam being alone with that Ximena woman?" Holly asked during a lull in business.

Smidgeon smiled. "No. Sam and I have an understanding about such things, so if he knows what's good for him, he'll keep to himself. Seriously, I trust him. And in a weird way, I trust her, too. Anyway, Ximena likes Lance."

"She does?"

"Oh, yes."

"Isn't she too young for him?"

"Maybe, but that's between those two. Sam says she's eighteen, but she seems a might worldly for that age, so I reckon it'll be okay."

A short time later, the café door opened and Sam walked in, followed by Ximena and Dave.

"Dave!" Holly ran to the door and embraced him. "You're okay?"

"I'll be as right as rain as soon as I have a shower and a hot meal."

"Might need to get those in reverse order. I'm Smidgeon; this is my place." She then turned to Sam and gave him a bear hug before kissing him. "About danged time you got back."

Lance emerged from the kitchen to see what the commotion was, then stopped and stared at Ximena, who approached him and took his hand.

"You know, you saved my life," he said.

"I *had* to," she said as she put her arms around him and hugged him. "I could not allow anything to happen to you because I know now that I love you."

"I thought you said..."

"Never mind what I said." She tilted her head and rose on her tiptoes to kiss him. "I'm just glad you are safe."

"Me, too."

Holly kissed Dave again and turned to go into the kitchen. "I'll go fix you something. You want something, Sam?"

"Sure, maybe just a pimento cheese sandwich."

"Okay, okay, reunion time is over," Smidgeon said. "We've got a café to run. Dave, you sit yourself down and eat. Lance, you look to be about the same size, do you think you could lend him something clean?"

"I, I," Lance stammered and glanced down at Ximena before saying, "uh, yeah, sure." He turned back to Smidgeon. "Of course. I'll make a quick run to my house."

"I will go with you," Ximena added.

Smidgeon tugged at Sam's sleeve. "Sam, we need to have a little talk."

"Sure," he said, and they went through the kitchen to the little office in back and closed the door.

"What's up?" he whispered.

"Bea called with some more information. She found a big piece of the puzzle. Rey Mendoza may well be Holly's father."

"What?"

"Holly didn't know before I told her. Bea found evidence indicating Mendoza had a daughter by a woman named Patrice Blanca. Holly freaked out when she overheard me talking to Bea and I repeated the name. Patrice is definitely Holly's mother, she verified it. We haven't mentioned anything to anyone else yet." Smidgeon took a deep breath. "Do you need to get cleaned up?"

"If I can splash some water on my face, I think I'll be good."

"So the exchange went okay?"

"Things got a little tense because they wanted Holly. I guess now we know why."

Smidgeon smirked. "Maybe, but I still can't figure out why it would matter."

After Sam washed his hands and face, he and Smidgeon returned to the dining room. Dave was eating and Holly pointed at another pimento cheese sandwich. "That one is yours, Sam."

As Sam sat and started to eat, Smidgeon asked Dave, "Why are they so intent on getting Holly?"

Dave swallowed a mouthful with a gulp. "I don't know anything about that. They've pretty much kept me under wraps since they grabbed me, but that was at least the third time they'd thrown me in that danged trunk. It was starting to feel like home."

Lance and Ximena returned with some clothes just as Dave finished eating. "Ain't nothing fancy," he said.

"I've been wearing the same rags for weeks. It will feel good to peel them off and wear something clean."

Smidgeon said, "Holly, why don't you take him over to the motel so he can get cleaned up?"

"Don't you need me for the lunch rush?"

"Sam's here, so we should be fine. I know you two have got some catching up to do."

"It would be great to grab some shut-eye in a real bed, too," Dave said.

"We'll get back as soon as we can," Holly added.

"But don't be too late. Mule is going to want to know everything."

"Mule?" Dave asked.

"He's a friend of ours, a private eye. He's been working with us on this case for weeks," Sam said.

"Yeah, he said he'd be along later for an early supper," Lance said. "When I was at the house, I told him what I knew, which wasn't much."

Mule arrived in the late afternoon and after eating, he sat quietly, drumming his fingers on the table the way he always did when he was pondering a situation. During a break, Sam and Smidgeon joined him.

"So they want Holly. Try as I might, I can't figure that one out," Mule said.

"We're pretty sure Holly is Rey Mendoza's daughter," Sam whispered.

"How in Sam Hill—did she know about this?"

Smidgeon shook her head. "No, not until I told her. Bea found out Mendoza had a daughter and told me the mother's name. Holly overheard me repeat the name and said it was *her* mother's name."

Sam added, "I guess Dave was their bargaining chip to get her to go willingly. Now that he's here, who knows what they will do to get her."

"That's just not enough reason to kidnap a person. I mean, a person will kidnap a blood-related child, but an adult? That's a new one on me. Still, from what we know, I think you're right. Who knows what they'll do next," Mule said. "When everyone gets here, I'll talk to Dave and see what else he knows."

"He said he doesn't know anything else," Sam said.

"He probably knows more than he realizes. There are always tiny details that don't seem important at the time."

"Once a cop, always a cop," Sam quipped.

"They should be along soon, then we can go over all of these things," Smidgeon suggested.

At seven-thirty, a car pulled into the parking lot. "Haven't had a customer in a half hour," Sam said. "I was hoping to run by the house real quick."

Smidgeon said, "Honey, you can run out if you need to."

The door opened and a woman walked in.

Smidgeon's mouth was wide open before she finally managed a meek, "Bea?"

"Something came up, and I decided you needed to see this right away. I thought it was quite important, so I didn't want to share it over the phone."

"Oh, my," Smidgeon said. "So you just drove in from El Paso? Come sit down. Coffee?"

"Actually, do you have hot tea?"

"Sure, I can fix you some hot tea. Milk?"

"Yes," she said, taking off her coat. "Spring cool front just came through, so it's a little chilly tonight. I came right over after getting a motel room but I'm starving. Is the kitchen open?"

Sam said, "Yes, we're still open."

"Then a burger would be nice as well."

"You bet. You got here just in time." Sam turned toward the kitchen.

Smidgeon brought Bea a steaming mug and a juice glass with a little milk in it. "You came at a really good time because we were fixing to discuss the latest developments, so you'll fit right in."

"There are other new developments?"

"A few."

"Then I'll wait. After you bring everyone up to date, I want them to hear about what I found."

Mule walked over from his seat in the corner. "Mind if I sit down? Name's Mule Hollis."

"I'm Bea Welbourne." She shook his outstretched hand. "Pleased to meet you. You have a very colorful name, Mule."

"Nickname. My given name is Mulvihill, Mule sort of came out of that."

"I think that's actually an Irish surname," she said.

"Exactly right, it's a family name."

Dave and Holly returned at eight and Bea was just finishing her last bite of food as Smidgeon locked the door behind them and placed the closed sign in the window.

Sam had pushed several tables together and they all sat as Smidgeon began. "First, for those of you who don't know her, this is Bea Welbourne. She's the librarian from UT El Paso who's been helping us. And this gentleman," she said pointing, "is Dave Adams. His disappearance is what started all of this." She proceeded to introduce the others to Bea and Dave. "The first bit of news I want to share is that Bea discovered that Rey Mendoza has a daughter by a woman named Patrice Blanca. We have since discovered that Patrice Blanca is Holly's mother.

Bea said, "I knew it was important, I just had no idea how important it was."

Lance jumped up, "That explains a lot!"

"But not everything," Mule said.

Holly blushed. "I had no idea until Smidgeon told me. I don't even know who this Mendoza character is. My parents never mentioned him at all."

Sam started. "Well, let's go through what we have and maybe we can figure it out."

Bea nodded. "You go on, Sam. I have new clues that will help, but I want to hear everything you have before I share what I found out today."

Sam glanced at Bea and raised one eyebrow, then continued. "Ximena and I went to Carlsbad to meet with the guys who kidnapped Dave. After a few tense words, we managed to trade the note for Dave's release. These were the same characters we faced off with in Lincoln when we rescued Lance."

"Wait, what note?" Bea asked.

"We'll get to that," Mule whispered in her ear.

"We know this has something to do with an old treasure that is possibly buried in the Capitan Mountains of New Mexico."

"And great evil," Ximena added.

Sam nodded at Ximena and continued. "We thought Dave was the key, but now we think it might be Holly. We don't know exactly why."

"Well, if Holly is Mendoza's daughter..." Lance said.

Mule interrupted him. "It's interesting, but it's not enough to warrant this much attention."

"I might have something to add to that." Bea stood and continued. "I've been intrigued by this story ever since Sam and Smidgeon came to me a few weeks ago. I'm a research librarian and I think I'm pretty good at my trade, so I have spent hours digging through every record I could find. My library has extensive holdings of documents from the time period that relates to this treasure. I recently found a very rare manuscript and I've been working to translate it."

"What is it?"

"It is a copy of the written transcript of Padre de la Garza's interrogation. As I translated it, I realized it wasn't something akin to a police interrogation, it was more a function of the Spanish Inquisition."

"Wasn't the Inquisition much earlier?" Sam asked.

"If the right conditions existed, it continued well into the nineteenth century," Bea said before continuing. "The Inquisition was known to be ruthless and, according to this record, Padre de la Garza cursed everyone who was acting against him, that is, until he finally succumbed to the tortures inflicted upon him, most notably something called *tortura del agua*, and another called *strappado*."

Smidgeon gasped. "Wow, neither of those sounds very pleasant."

"They weren't." Bea continued, "The first involves putting a cloth in one's mouth and then dribbling water into it to simulate drowning."

"Gives me the shivers," Smidgeon said.

"In the second one, the person has their hands and arms bound behind their back and they are lifted by the bound hands backwards and suspended."

"Ouch. That would be it for me," Lance said, "I'd tell them whatever they wanted to know."

Bea smiled. "The good padre apparently endured it in silence. He didn't say a word until they applied hot coals to the soles of his feet while he was suspended. His crimes were against both the church and the crown, so they felt justified using these extreme measures in order to get a confession."

"Okay, we get the idea," Sam said. "So he finally broke."

"Well, according to what I read, he didn't completely break. At least not in the way they expected, but he did tell them about some of the things we are already familiar with.

The circle of boulders, for instance. But he said they moved many of those the rocks to try to make a defensive wall instead."

Lance asked, "So it would have been a line of big rocks?"

"Yes, along one side. A semicircle on the other. They were attacked before they completed it."

Lance looked at the others. "I saw a line of rocks but walked right past it because I was looking for a circle. I think I was there."

"If I might go on," Bea said looking over the top of her glasses. "They proceeded up the arroyo to the *gruta*, which means grotto. This is the second time I have seen this reference. It's confusing. It seems to me that the arid landscape in that area wouldn't have anything like a grotto."

Sam chimed in, "Probably a distinctive landmark in the arroyo wall. In the dark it might have reminded them of a grotto."

"Perhaps," Bea said. "He blessed the location in honor of the feast of St. Michael and they returned to the spot one last time before their planned escape. They hoped to get away in the growing darkness as the lunar eclipse progressed. This was when they saw what he termed *el milagro*—the miracle."

"Now this is getting more interesting," Smidgeon said.

"The padre said he had a vision at this point and an archangel he assumed was Saint Michael appeared to him and cast a special shadow on the wall in the faint light of the penumbra, directly above the spot where they buried their cache of booty. Both he and Mendoza saw it, but their associates didn't. Due to their shared vision, he assumed only they or their descendants would be able to see the location again, and only during the penumbra of an eclipse."

"Wow," Sam said.

"And Holly is..." Smidgeon started.

Holly stood and interrupted. "I guess from what we've learned, I'm a direct descendent of Diego Mendoza."

Eight mouths dropped at once.

"That explains a whole heck of a lot," Mule said.

"Yeah, the hidden figure on the note for one thing," Sam added.

"And Holly is almost the only person..." Smidgeon started.

Sam finished, "Who will be able to see it. Ever. The padre likely has no direct descendants."

Lance rubbed his chin and speculated. "That's right. Catholic priests are celibate."

"Supposed to be," Sam reminded Lance.

"I have one last detail to share," Bea said.

"Oh, man, I'm not sure I can take any more," Lance said.

"I couldn't help but look it up. There is an eclipse of the moon coming in two weeks. April twenty-fourth. I don't know what you all want to do about that fact, but whatever it is, I'm in."

Mule's reply was grim. "Whatever we know, *they* probably know most of it as well and it explains why they need Holly."

Eighteen

"So, what *are* we going to do?" Mule asked the assembled group.

Lance was first to speak. "I'm up for going out there. Any thought of treasure is exciting, but after everything I've been through, I know one thing for sure. I don't want those guys to get it."

"I don't know enough about their motivations to draw any conclusions about the treasure," Mule said.

Dave leaned forward. "This other fella is right; they want the treasure. It's all they talked about. They work for a guy who knows details about it nobody else knows."

"Rey Mendoza," Smidgeon said. "Holly's father."

"What does he need those two thugs for?" Mule asked.

Smidgeon answered, "Bea told me he's paralyzed."

"Yes, that's what I read," Bea affirmed.

"So, he needs the muscle," Lance said. "There's no way he could ever get out there on his own."

"Let's say we find this treasure before they do," Mule said, "It's most likely on private or Federal land. We'd have no claim to it."

Sam leaned back in his chair. "Unless it could be pulled out without anybody knowing. That was my plan for years when I was treasure hunting."

Smidgeon shot him a withering glare. "You aren't going anywhere on that bad leg."

"Listen, it's sore, but the doc said I could do almost anything I'd normally do as long as I don't push it too hard."

"I've done a bit of backpacking, so maybe I can help," Bea said. "I must confess, I've been intrigued from the start. In the meantime, I can research the land and legal questions you've raised. I have to head back early in the morning, but I can schedule some vacation time around the date of the eclipse." She pulled a pocket planner from her purse and flipped pages. "It's a Thursday."

Lance said, "I'm pretty sure I was right on top of it the last time I went out there, so I know the route in. It's not a walk in the park, but I think Sam would probably do okay. Heck, I think even Mule could make it."

Mule said, "Not sure I'm up for gallivanting off into the wilderness, but I could stay in reserve and watch your backs." He leaned forward. "Understand this...they probably know about the eclipse. That means they're probably desperate to get Holly, so she's got to stay hidden until then."

"I'm no hiker," she said. "You expect me to go off with you into those mountains?"

Dave took her by the hand. "Baby, if what we heard here today is true, you're maybe the only one who can see it."

"But I don't care about this stupid treasure. I don't know this Rey Mendoza, and I don't care if he is my real father. I don't care about any of this. I just wanted you back and now that you're here, I want it to be over."

Smidgeon stood. "And seriously, I guess that is an option. You and Dave can leave and no one around here would know anything more about you. I don't much care about any treasure either. It's exciting and all, but I've got a business to run." She looked over at Sam and Lance. "You two, I know you both and know you've still got that bug, what do you call it?"

"The fever," Sam said.

"Right, but listen to me, none of us needs any of this trouble."

"We've got a while to think about it," Dave said. "But even if we find it, how much could it be worth?"

"If it's even still there," Sam added. "Three hundred years is a long time."

Ximena sat quietly through the discussion but at this point, she uttered one word, "Penumbra."

"What? Yeah, we know about that now," Dave said.

"You all must understand. I don't know about this eclipse you talk about, but I can see that the word is a spell of protection and this is the reason no one has found it. We need her," she said, pointing at Holly, "not to find the treasure but to help break the spell."

"Could *you* break it?" Sam asked.

Ximena lowered her eyes. "I do not know. Perhaps. Given time."

"So do we do it or not?" Bea asked.

Smidgeon responded. "I vote against. What do the rest of you say? Raise your hands if you want to pursue this foolishness."

Sam, Lance, Dave, and Bea raised their hands.

Sam looked around the room. "Four for, four against."

"Great," Dave said. "I'm really for just me going out there and taking my chances."

"You will never break the spell alone," Ximena said. "I need to spend some time thinking about all that has occurred. The thing none of you realize is that there is great evil attached to this spell. If it can be broken, perhaps the evil will be broken as well, but the evil one is very strong, I can feel it."

"But you voted against going," Lance said.

"Yes. I think it is foolish to unnecessarily confront evil. The danger is great...its power will be greater during the penumbra."

"Hogwash," Mule said.

Ximena's eyes smoldered at Mule. "Just because you do not believe in things you do not understand does not mean they do not exist."

"Well, unless something happens to change anybody's mind, I think that is it," Smidgeon said. "Holly, I'll pay you for your time, but I think at the very least you and Dave need to take off and go someplace else, like El Paso, Fort Stockton, or anyplace as long as it is far away from here. I do think those goons will assume you're still here and they'll try to grab you."

"She's right," Dave said. "I voted to go, but maybe it's time to fold our cards and get out of town. I had a lot of time to think while they had me. They suckered me and somehow figured out I was a way to get to her. Even though they were in prison, this Mendoza guy put them up to it. I know he's the brains behind the whole deal."

"I've read that he's rich," Bea said, "and has a lot of connections."

"If he's rich, why does he need a treasure?" Smidgeon asked.

Mule smiled. "Ever seen a rich person that didn't want to get even richer?"

"Plus, there's a family connection," Bea added. "He has grown up hearing tales about Diego Mendoza and this treasure, things that have been passed down for generations. He thinks he is entitled to it."

"And with his disability, Holly is his only means of getting it," Sam added. "I agree, the treasure is secondary, and, Holly, if you don't care about that, you need to get away for your own good. They're coming after you, and they don't have much time."

"There is one thing you haven't considered," Bea said.

"What?"

"A lunar eclipse is a regular event, usually a couple of times a year. This year there will be another one in October, the seventeenth, I think."

Holly turned to Dave. "Then this is never going to be over. We need to leave like Smidgeon said. Let's get out of here tonight."

"I'll protect you as best as I can," Dave said.

Smidgeon got up and went to her office. "I'll get you your wages. Cash. Plus a bonus. You'll need it."

"I guess that's it then," Lance said.

~ * ~

A loud banging on the front door woke Sam out of a dead sleep.

"What is it?" Smidgeon asked sleepily.

"Somebody's at the door."

Sam pulled on a T-shirt and pants and hurried to the door. It was Clay Dodge from the sheriff's office.

"Sorry to wake you up."

"Is there anything wrong?"

"Trouble at the Dolings Motel. Miss Holly was kidnapped right out of her room. Looked like she put up quite a fight. I feel just awful, Sam. She was always just as nice as she could be to me."

"So somebody grabbed Holly?"

"She had a gentleman friend with her. He tried to fight them, too, but the attackers shot him. He's pretty bad off and being transported to El Paso."

"That is probably Dave Adams. Holly's boyfriend."

"So you know him?"

"Just met him."

"Any idea what all of this is about?"

"I'll level with you," Sam said. "Dave Adams is an ex-con. He's had some trouble with a couple of former inmates he knew. Holly had some history with Smidgeon, so she came down here to get away from some of that drama."

"Apparently it wasn't far enough away. But that doesn't explain why they'd kidnap her."

"Maybe Dave can explain that."

"If he makes it. I guess it was wishful thinking to imagine all this sort of stuff was behind you guys."

"I know it always seems that way, but we're as much in the dark about this as you. She just worked for us, that's all."

"Okay, if you think of anything else, you know where we are."

"Sure, Clay."

Sam turned around after closing the door and Smidgeon was standing behind him.

"I heard most of it."

"Not good. I thought she was leaving last night."

"I did, too."

They sat on the couch. "I better call Lance and Mule," Sam said.

"I guess this changes everything." Smidgeon frowned.

Sam gravely added, "Yeah. Well, there isn't any way we leave her to the wolves on the twenty-fourth, is there?"

"No, I guess not," Smidgeon said.

Headlights reflected past the window. "Somebody else here," Sam said.

Smidgeon went to the door and saw Bea hurrying across the yard. "Horrible news," she said. "I was sound asleep at the motel when I heard a fight, then gunshots. Holly was kidnapped and Dave was shot. I didn't know what else to do, so I thought I had better come right over."

"We already heard. How'd you find us?"

"I looked you up; you're in the phone book. What do we do now?"

"Sam's calling Mule and Lance."

"And that other young woman? Ximena?"

"I don't know where she might be."

Bea leaned forward and whispered, "She's a *bruja*, isn't she?"

"Something like that. I can't explain the things she knows or does but she freaks me out."

"I can see that. I helped a professor research *brujería* a while back. I read some pretty strange things."

Sam hung up the phone as they came into the living room. "Mule is heading to the motel and Lance is coming right over."

"I'll put on a pot of coffee," Smidgeon said.

"I guess this changes things," Bea said. "I assume we're going out there for the eclipse?"

Smidgeon sighed. "I don't see that we have any other choice."

"They'll kill Holly after they find the treasure," Sam said. "The only way we can possibly save her is to beat them out there and set up an ambush."

Bea leaned forward. "Isn't it time to get the police involved?"

Sam shook his head. "Tough question. Ideally, yes. But in this case, they aren't going to buy all this penumbra business. And don't forget about Earl and Ding. If they see the police, they'll just wait it out until the next eclipse. Who knows what might happen to Holly in the meantime?"

"I see what you mean," Bea said. "So we need to go out there."

"Some of us," Sam said.

"Not you!" Smidgeon bellowed.

"We'll see."

There was a knock on the door and Sam limped hurriedly to open it. "Hi, Lance."

"Sounds like there's been a lot of foolishness tonight," he said as he took off his hat and coat. "Oh, hi, Bea."

"I was at the motel and heard the commotion. I heard the gunshot, too."

"So they took Holly," Lance said.

"And shot Dave," Smidgeon added.

"Lordy. Mule went to see if he could find out anything else. He'll check in here when he's done."

Sam brought four cups of coffee from the kitchen. "We're talking about changing the plans. I think these events have broken our stalemate."

Lance cradled the steaming cup in both hands. "Yeah, I agree with that."

"Sam doesn't think we should involve the police," Bea said.

"At this point, that's probably a wise notion."

"That's probably Mule," Lance said after they all heard a car door.

The front doorknob rattled before Sam could get to it. "Hold on," he said.

Mule stood on the small porch holding his hat. "Figured with everybody here it would be unlocked."

"Not with kidnappers lurking about."

Mule entered the living room and nodded to the assembly. "Howdy, folks." He placed his hat on a side table and sat on a dining room chair Sam had brought over. "They were just about wrapping up by the time I got there. Not much to see. But I did get one piece of news."

"What's that?" Sam asked.

He said, "It wasn't good news either. I was sorry to hear this, but Dave died in the ambulance."

"Oh, my," Bea said.

Lance jumped to his feet and waved both arms in alarm. "So now it's murder as well as kidnapping."

Smidgeon held one hand to her chest. "Poor Holly. She must already be traumatized, but this news will surely devastate her."

Mule tapped his fingers on the brim of his Stetson. "This puts everything in a new perspective. We now know beyond the shadow of a doubt they are willing to kill."

"Dang," Lance said, "and they were supposedly his friends."

"Friends who had already kidnapped him once before. Any idea which way they went?" Sam asked.

"Well, they could have gone anywhere. Mexico is close, and I'm sure that's what the police are thinking. But knowing what we know, I imagine they're heading north to New Mexico." Mule lowered his head. "I'm going to head up that way just as soon as we finish up here."

"We're thinking the plan to go find the treasure is back on."

"I figured as much. I won't be much use out there, but I can work with you in the background."

"Where you headed?"

"I just want to follow a feeling in my gut. I'll be at the Smoky Bear Motel again, in Capitan."

"Mitch Blalock?" Lance asked.

"Exactly. I want to see what he knows about Rey Mendoza."

"Yeah," Lance said. "Funny he never mentioned that name, him being such an expert and all."

Bea spoke up. "Oh, there is a local expert on the Archangel treasure?"

"Yes. At least he calls himself one. Runs a curio shop up in Capitan."

"Has anybody seen Ximena since we left the cafe?" Lance asked.

Everyone shook their heads.

"I hope she's okay," he said.

Sam responded, "If there is one person in our group who is probably safe, it's Ximena."

Nineteen

Mule mused, "New Mexico is starting to grow on me. Maybe I'll retire up here someday."

He stopped in Roswell and discussed updates over a cup of coffee with Detective Michaels.

"Our friends Earl and Ding are the likely suspects in a murder and kidnapping down your way," Michaels said. "I heard they grabbed Holly Slidell."

"Yep. That's the reason I came back up here."

"I thought you were going to call me if you found anything on David Adams."

"I was, but I only learned he was down there last night, right before he was killed. I was going to call you today."

Michaels sipped his coffee. "So do you think she was nabbed by Earl and Ding?"

"Yeah, I'm pretty sure they did it, but I also have a line on who they might be working for."

"Rey Mendoza?" Michaels asked.

"That's the guy. You told me he was some kind of crime boss."

"He's got his fingers in a lot of things. Besides crime, he's rich and well connected. Politically, I mean."

"I'm familiar with the type, working both sides of the fence, legal and illegal."

"Why would you think Mendoza is involved?"

"He has a family connection to the Archangel Cache. Oh, and there's another minor detail...Holly Slidell is his daughter."

Michaels' jaw dropped. "What?"

"She was given up for adoption when she was a baby, but we're pretty darn sure she's his daughter. I have a researcher over at University of Texas El Paso who's been looking things up for m—she dug up that tidbit. She's really good."

"Why would a guy have his own daughter kidnapped?"

"That's the big question, isn't it?" Mule sipped his coffee. "Dave Adams was pretty sure Mendoza was after his daughter all along."

"So I guess you're up here looking for them."

"That's about the size of it. I also wanted to look a little more into Mendoza's connection to all of this."

"Well, understand, we're on the lookout for them, too. The feds don't think they'd come here because too many people know all three of them. My captain agrees. He thinks they went to Mexico."

"I figure they're headed up toward the Capitan area," Mule said.

"Back up there? Interesting idea, I guess, but I'd be careful if I were you. If Rey Mendoza is involved, you can be sure he's covering all his bases. And Mule..."

"Yeah?"

"You should let the police handle it. Seriously. These guys have committed at least two capital crimes that we know of, and there is no way a lone, unlicensed investigator can do as much as we can."

Mule tapped his fingers on the table. "I know."

"At least call me if you find anything."

"I will, but it ain't as if I can pick up my car phone, you know."

Michaels chuckled.

After they parted ways, Mule drove to Capitan and checked into The Smoky Bear.

Recognition flashed on the clerk's face when she saw the name on the room registration. "Oh, Mr. Hollis? I think I have a message waiting for you." She fumbled with some papers, "Here it is, Mulvihill Hollis?"

"That's me," he smirked as he grabbed the note. Bea Welbourne wanted him to call her and she had left a number. He looked at the clock and saw it was four forty-five. "Can I call from the room?"

"Yes, sir, there's a charge."

"There always is."

He got the key and hurried to his room. He immediately dropped his briefcase and dialed the number.

"Special Collections, Bea Welbourne speaking."

"Bea, this is Mule Hollis. I was surprised to get your message."

"Oh, yes. You just caught me." He could hear papers rustling over the phone. "I remembered that at one point you said you were going up there and mentioned the name of the motel in Capitan. I hope you don't mind."

"Not at all. What's up?"

"Well, you talked about a man named Mitch Blalock who runs a curio shop in Capitan. I did some research on him."

"You are persistent. I like that."

"It's what I do. Mitch Blalock is not the owner of that curio shop. I had a friend in New Mexico check it out for me."

"He doesn't own it?"

"No, it's owned by Rey Mendoza. I thought you'd want that bit of information before you start asking him any questions."

Mule took a second to stare at the handset and wondered to himself, "Who *is* this woman?"

"Are you there?"

"I had to take a moment to let that sink in. You are absolutely right. That is a very valuable piece of information. Thank you very much Mrs..." Mule felt his face flush.

"Not Mrs.," she said.

"I should have said Bea."

"Yes, please call me Bea. I'll keep digging, but I'm sure I'll see you soon. I've put in for some vacation time around the time of the eclipse. This is all quite thrilling."

"Might be dangerous. These people are ruthless."

"I take it you don't know many librarians."

"No, ma'am, I don't."

"You should disregard the stereotype. I, for one, thrive on a little excitement. I'll let you know if I find anything more. Call if you need my help." She gave Mule her home number.

"I will."

He put the handset down and mused to himself, "So Mitch Blalock is in cahoots with Rey Mendoza."

~ * ~

"Sam, honey, you are not going, and that's all there is to it. You aren't going!"

"But..."

"No buts. What are we going to do if that rod in your leg starts acting up and you are two hours into a hike? What good are you going to be to Holly or any of us?"

"So you're going?"

"Yes, I plan on taking your place. You know I can take care of myself. And besides, I'm responsible for Holly."

"How are you responsible?"

"If I hadn't met her up in Roswell, she wouldn't have come here and asked *me* for help."

"At least let me try hiking a little around here, to test my leg. I think I can do it."

"I'll agree to that, but no more than a mile, okay? Baby steps."

"Okay. I guess we had better go open the café," Sam said.

Smidgeon hugged Sam then kissed him. "I know I worry about you, but you think you're a superhero. Sam, even superheroes have to let their danged broken bones heal."

Sam sighed. "You're right. You're always right."

"And don't you forget it!"

On the way to the restaurant, Sam broached the other detail they had not discussed. "We haven't talked about the restaurant. Do we close?"

"You can run it," she said.

"I know I can run it, but what if we both go out there? I mean, we close for Christmas and Easter and we closed for that little expedition to rescue Lance, but how many times can we close like that without hurting ourselves financially?"

"Not many. One of us should stay...I'm still leaning toward you."

"What if my little walking tests show I can make it?"

"We'll cross that bridge if we need to, but I think you're only fooling yourself. You think you're getting along all right, but you don't see yourself gimp around the dining room. Lordy, Sam, you can't even push in the clutch on Loot's truck without wincing in pain."

"Well, it's a particularly tight clutch."

"Convenient excuse. Look, you'd probably help us better by staying."

"Like you said, we'll cross that bridge when we get to it."

The lights were on when they arrived. "Lance must already be here," Smidgeon said.

He had three cups of coffee sitting on a table when they walked in.

"Couldn't sleep," Lance said, "So I came in and did the prep work."

Sam asked, "Any word from Ximena?"

"I haven't seen or heard from her since the last meeting with Dave. The danged house was just too lonely with Mule gone up to New Mexico." Lance was pacing back and forth.

"Aw, Lance. Why don't you just sit down?"

"Too restless," he said.

"I haven't ever seen you like this, buddy," Sam said.

"Haven't felt like this in a long time," he said. "I'm worried about her, what with those killers and all. She showed them up once..."

"Twice," Sam corrected. "But trust me, they're afraid of her and you should know something else that is even more important."

"What's that?"

"She can take care of herself. I've seen it."

Lance sat, sipped his coffee and said, "Of course, you're right. I just got it bad, Sam. You don't think she's cast a spell on me or something, do you?"

Sam burst out in laughter, then composed himself. "I hadn't thought of that, but no. Don't forget, I spent hours with her. She likes you, buddy, and she knows you like her.

Any spell she might have cast on you doesn't have anything to do with magic."

"And she's so young, that's another thing that bothers me."

"She's eighteen going on sixty, if you ask me," Smidgeon said.

Sam added. "So what if you are a little older?"

"Just be careful...you don't know anything about her." Smidgeon added, "Still, as much as I hate all this witchy business, I like the girl. I really do. She's growing on me."

~ * ~

Mule spent some time driving around the small confines of Capitan after breakfast on the off chance he might catch a glimpse of Earl Rector, Ding Stewart, or their stolen Mercury.

"I'm spending too much danged time on not making any money," he grumbled to himself. "And that car's probably been replaced by another stolen one."

He finally parked in front of the curio shop. It looked closed, but the sign said it opened at ten.

Mule looked at his watch. "Ten minutes late," he whispered, "but it's off-season and these small towner folks like to keep their own hours."

A few minutes later, he heard a click and could see a hand through the dingy glass as it flipped the sign. He got out and entered the store.

Mitch Blalock didn't even turn around. "I saw the car and knew it was you." He got behind the counter and faced Mule. "Don't know what else I can tell you."

"Tell me about Rey Mendoza."

Blalock tried to conceal his surprise by stammering, "Uh, uh, er, he's, uh, he's my landlord. W-What do you need to know? I d-don't know anything else about him."

"Your landlord? I've heard he's more than that."

"Not sure what you mean."

"Doesn't he flat out own this business? You work for *him*, right?"

"Well, in a manner of speaking."

"It was a yes or no question."

"Look, I'm within my rights to ask you to leave this place right now."

"Did you know he was behind a kidnapping and a murder?"

"Wha...?"

"That's right. Down in Texas. Two men grabbed a girl named Holly Slidell from her motel room and hauled her into a waiting car. Her boyfriend tried to fight the men and they shot and killed him. Those men also work for your boss, Rey Mendoza."

"Look, Rey was a friend of my father's. He sort of let me run this place to keep me out of trouble when I got clean, off of heroin. I've gotten used to the slow pace here. I try to make more than I need to live on and anything extra goes to Rey. I don't know nothing about any of that other stuff."

"Do you know of his connection to the Archangel Cache?"

Again Blalock faltered slightly as he said, "Y-yes. He's a direct descendent of Diego Mendoza."

Mule's investigatory mind clicked and he remembered a detail from their previous conversation. He was sure Blalock had never mentioned Diego's last name when he was originally telling the story. It was proof that Blalock had been holding back.

"But," Blalock continued, "I can't believe Mister Mendoza would murder or kidnap anyone."

"It might have been helpful to tell us the survivor of the Archangel party had a living descendent."

"I didn't think it was relevant, and besides, he's a very private person and he doesn't want anything to do with it. Heck, it probably isn't even out there. It's a story to tell the tourists, you know, to get them to spend money."

"Do you believe that?"

Blalock dropped his chin to his chest. "I honestly don't know."

"Finally the truth," Mule said. "But I know one thing...after I leave, I know you'll probably grab the phone and tell him I was here. You can tell him I'm onto him and I'll be danged if I'll let anybody else get hurt."

Blalock pointed toward the door. "I think you should leave."

Mule stood outside and put his sunglasses on. "That went just about the way I expected," he muttered, as he slammed the car door and drove off.

~ * ~

Sam sat alone on the couch with MamaKat. He'd snapped awake and couldn't go back to sleep, so he went out to be alone with his thoughts. As he petted the cat, she tensed and growled.

A wispy figure was lightly glowing on the other end of the couch. "There's trouble brewing."

"Hello, Loot. Yes, lots of trouble."

"I've tried to make my way up to where you folks are going, but something keeps blocking me. Maybe once you head up there, I'll be swept along with you. It's happened before."

"What's it like for you?"

"Ain't bad. To tell the truth, it ain't much of nothing. Nothing I know how to explain."

"I appreciate you keeping an eye on me."

"I've tried to help you when I could. It takes a lot out of me. You just be careful, you hear? We're both dealing with something outside my experience."

Sam squinted in the dark room, but the shadowy presence had faded. MamaKat relaxed and resumed a deep and relentless purr.

Twenty

Members of the small group congregated in Lance's living room on the morning before the April eclipse. Lance and Sam sat on kitchen chairs, while Smidgeon and Bea sat on the couch.

"Why did Mule go back to New Mexico?" Bea asked. "I mean, I knew he went once to confront that curio shop owner about his connection to Rey Mendoza, but I thought he came home, didn't he?"

"He had business to attend to down here."

"And now he's up there again?"

"He's doing background work before we go up. You know, scouting around to find us access routes and such. He also has a contact who can let him know if Earl and Ding have been spotted," Sam said.

"So the three of us will go up in my car, right?" she said.

"If you don't mind. Your Cherokee is big enough to carry us and our equipment," Lance said.

"I'll stay with the car," Sam said. "You three will head up the trail."

"I hope those walkie-talkies we bought work." Lance walked to a front-facing window and looked out. "I can't believe Ximena has been gone so long...almost two weeks." He turned around. "You think they got ahold of her?"

Smidgeon said, "I know you're worried about her, but I'm sure she's fine."

"Anyway, we don't have room for her and we don't want to take two vehicles...it's too noticeable."

Sam asked, "Where do we meet Mule again?"

Bea and Lance answered in unison. "The Smoky Bear Motel in Capitan."

"How do we get ourselves into these situations?" Smidgeon asked.

Sam joked, "Hey, this one's on you. You're the one with the connection to Holly."

"I guess you're right. And to think this all started because Dave was missing, yet now he's dead."

"Well," Lance added, "if we want to have any chance at all of helping Holly, we need to do this."

"What about your dog, Lance?"

"Neighbor lady will feed her and take her out for me."

Sam added, "MamaKat should be okay for a few days. I've left her a ton of food and water."

"The car's loaded," Sam said, "and the 'family emergency' sign is on the door of the café. I guess after I call Mule, we're ready to lock up and head out."

Once they were all in the car, Bea headed out to the main road with Smidgeon in the passenger seat giving her directions.

"We appreciate all of your help, Bea," Smidgeon said. "You know, you don't have to do this."

"Of course I do. I love a good caper and this one is better than most. Hey, I'm a librarian, I know all about solving mysteries."

"But you're using up your vacation time."

"I have plenty saved up. The truth is, my life has been stodgy and boring lately. I've hardly been away from my job for over a year, so this will do me good."

"There may be danger, though."

"Makes it all the more exciting." Bea glanced at Smidgeon. "I don't have a gun, so I guess I should ask, does anybody else? I would assume these gentlemen we're going to meet are armed."

"I always carry a gun in my boot," Lance said.

"And I've got my daddy's forty-five," Smidgeon added, patting her purse.

"I don't have one," Sam said.

"Okay, then, that at least gives us some firepower on our side."

The time passed quickly with smatterings of friendly conversation, but they all grew quiet and pensive as the car approached their destination.

Around mid-afternoon, Smidgeon quoted the sign announcing, "Capitan."

"Should be up just a little way," Lance said, adding a few minutes later, "there it is, and there's Mule's car outside the restaurant."

"We should grab a bite anyway," Sam added.

Lance opened the door for the others. "The food's pretty good at this place."

They spotted Mule sitting in a corner booth big enough to accommodate them all. "I guessed right, you guys made good time. I've only been sitting here about ten minutes."

"How long does it take from here?" Bea asked.

"Not too long," Mule answered. "Lance probably knows that better than me."

"Less than an hour. Your Cherokee should handle it better than my truck did."

"Everybody eat a good meal," Mule said. "This is likely going to be a long night."

After they ordered, Mule continued. "Bea told me the eclipse will begin about ten and run about five hours."

"Yes, but we've heard again and again about the penumbra. The penumbra phase of an eclipse is only during the first part and the last part, and I'm not sure how long it lasts."

"And we're supposed to be able to see something during that, right?" Smidgeon asked.

"Well, based on Bea's research, the theory is *Holly* should be able to see it," Sam corrected.

"Bea, Smidgeon and I will be there," Lance said, "and hopefully we can surprise them and get her away from them."

"And the Archangel Cache?" Bea asked.

"It's secondary to Holly," Sam said.

"That's right," Smidgeon said, "because we know once she sees whatever she is supposed to see, she will have completely served her purpose."

"They'll kill her, pure and simple," Sam said. "For us, tonight, she is the treasure."

"If they even show up," Lance said. "This is all just a guess."

"Well, it's not practical for them to hold her another six months until the next eclipse. After all, Earl and Ding are suspects in a murder." Sam sipped his glass of water. "Whether the story Bea found is true or not, we're pretty sure they're following the same scenario. The fact that they grabbed her so close to the event is a good indicator that we are all on the same track."

"I guess you're right."

Mule said, "So, after you eat, I suggest you all head out. I'll hold down the fort here."

Sam said, "I'll drop them off at the trailhead and find a spot away from it to park and monitor the radio."

~ * ~

A short time later, Lance said, "I remember I parked somewhere along here." He then pointed and said, "There's the trailhead."

Sam stopped the car and all four got out.

"Looks rough," Smidgeon observed.

"Yeah," Sam said. "As much as I'm itching to head down that trail, I'm afraid I'd end up being a liability. I tried to test it, but every time I walked a few hundred yards, my leg started to act up."

Lance said, "It's okay, Sam. We need somebody to monitor the radio and get help if we need it."

"Won't be quick help. I'd have to drive back down quite a distance to find a phone."

Bea started unloading the packs and Lance moved over to help her.

"So you live with Mule, right?" she asked.

"Yeah, I share that house with him. He runs his business out of the third bedroom."

"So he's not married?"

"Widower," Lance said. "Why?" he asked, straightening up.

"He just seems nice, you know?" she said. "I was just curious."

"I should have known it...you're sweet on him."

Bea blushed. "I don't know about that. But I do know you're attracted to that young woman who was at the café the last time I came to Van Horn."

"Ximena? Yeah, and I'm not ashamed to admit it either."

The three of them hoisted their packs and started down the trail, but the shortest, Smidgeon, turned around and went back to the car. Sam had been standing, watching them leave, and she embraced him and they shared a lingering kiss.

"You be careful out there," he said. "Call me and I'll get up there to help as best as I can."

"Hey, you ever know me to not be careful?"

"Well, you make sure Bea and Lance are careful."

She touched her first two fingers to her lips then reached them up to Sam's lips. "I love you."

"I love you, too. Now you better catch up before they lose you."

~ * ~

Mule was watching the television in his room when there was a faint tapping sound at the door. He opened it and was amazed to see the petite figure of Ximena.

"*Señor* Mule, we must help them."

"What are you talking about?"

"Penumbra is tonight...Lance and the two women face great danger."

Mule's eyes widened. "How could you know about that?"

Ximena took in a deep breath and exhaled slowly. "I have seen it."

"They're trying to save the other woman, Holly."

"*Si*, I see her, too. They will all be engulfed by the great evil."

"Come in and tell me more about it."

"No, we must leave now."

"I'm expecting somebody. I can't leave now."

"*Si*, a policeman. I know about this as well."

"Then you know I need to wait for him."

"This man, you trust him?"

"Yes, I do. He's a detective from Roswell."

"Then we wait," she said. She pushed past Mule and sat down.

"So what is this evil?"

"A spirit...a very old spirit who protects the treasure and he is at his most powerful during the penumbra."

"The eclipse."

"I do not know what that is."

"There is an eclipse of the moon tonight. The moon will be covered by the shadow of the earth. As I understand it, the penumbra is part of the eclipse."

Ximena nodded. "That is good to know."

"Where have you been? Lance has been worried about you."

She smiled. "That is sweet. He is a good man. It would upset me if something happened to him. That is why haste is so important. I am new to *brujeria*. For many summers, after I finished regular schooling in Texas, I went to Mexico to train with a friend of my *tia abuela*. She would often have me drive her to meet this man. She continued my training and trained me well, but even she would consult this *brujo* when she needed to. He is very powerful and knowing. I am still a novice, so I went to see this man, to ask him about my feeling for Lance."

"So your great aunt, your *tia abuela*, taught you the ways of *brujeria*."

"Yes, *Señor* Mule, it is my life now."

"What did this *brujo* tell you about your feelings?"

"He said true love could strengthen my power and he saw true love in my heart."

"Well, then, as soon as Detective Michaels gets here, I guess we'll follow after them. I was going to take him up there anyway. I thought the three of them might need some help."

"They do need help. I will go with you."

They sat in silence for fifteen more minutes until there was another knock at the door.

"Okay, you talked me into coming out of my jurisdiction," Michaels started, "what is this all about?"

"I have information that Earl Rector and Ding Stewart are taking Holly Slidell out into the wilderness tonight."

"Why on earth would they do that?"

"At the bidding of an evil presence," Ximena interrupted.

Michaels raised one eyebrow. "Who's this?"

"This," Mule said, pointing with his thumb, "is Ximena. She may be the key to solving this whole deal." Mule explained her part in the situation.

"Seriously? We're depending on some sort of folk witchcraft to help us?"

"I can't explain it, but she's got a feeling about what's at stake, and I have to admit I've learned she's usually right."

"Well, okay, the more the merrier, I guess. We'll take my car, okay? I have some additional firepower in the trunk if we need it."

As they drove to the trailhead, they continued to discuss the situation they were facing.

Michaels asked, "So there's some kind of magic involved with tonight's eclipse?"

"That's the way this legend operates, as near as we've been able to figure out."

"People have looked for the Archangel Cache for almost three hundred years."

"I know, but they didn't know it could only be found during the penumbra phase of a lunar eclipse."

"That's crazy."

"Maybe. But maybe not. There could be some trick to the light that occurs only during that time."

"But isn't it dark?"

"That's what I thought, but a researcher we've been working with told us the penumbra is the outer shadow, when the moon is partially darkened but not fully covered."

"Sam is near," Ximena said from the back seat

Michael's cocked his head. "Who the heck is Sam?"

"Another one of our group. He was going to stay back and keep their car out of sight." Mule turned back to her, "Do you know where?"

She inhaled deeply, as if she were sniffing the air, then said, "*Gira a la derecha. Aquí!*"

"Huh?" Michaels said.

Mule pointed and said, "We need to turn down this path to the right." Michaels made the turn. They saw a Jeep Cherokee parked in a small clearing.

Sam got out of the other car as they opened their doors and Mule approached him.

Sam said, "Didn't expect to see you tonight."

"Sam, this is Detective Michaels from Roswell."

Then a smaller figure became visible to Sam.

"Ximena! We've been wondering where you were."

Mule pointed at her. "She convinced me we needed to come up here and help. She doesn't think those three will be able to handle the evil one, as she calls him."

Michaels squinted at the sky. "It's getting dark, how are we supposed to get up there if we can't see? And what about you, Mule? These trails are rough. Can you take it?"

"I doubt it."

"Sam will go," Ximena said. "And you, *señor*," she said, pointing at Michaels. "I will lead you both."

"Not sure my leg will take it."

"You *must* go. I will help you."

Something in the tone of her voice compelled Sam. "Okay, the trailhead is back down to the main path, then up about fifty yards."

Michaels opened his trunk and pulled out two pump shotguns. "Police issue. These will stop just about anything." He also extracted a small knapsack. "I had a feeling there might be a hike involved. Got some water, extra ammo, and a little food."

Sam tested his leg. "I guess we'll see if this thing holds up."

"What do you mean?"

"Sam here is recovering from a broken leg."

Michaels looked him up and down and shook his head. "You sure you want to do this?"

Sam looked over at Ximena's stern expression then back to Michaels. "I don't think I have a choice."

Mule asked, "Should we call the others and let them know we're coming?"

"We agreed to keep radio silence except for an emergency," Sam said. "We were afraid if we chattered too much the others might hear us, either by their own radios or by the noise."

Sam handed Mule the walkie-talkie. "I guess you're up."

Twenty-one

Lance squinted through the glare of the afternoon sun and spotted the row of rocks he had seen before. "That's it, I'm sure of it," he whispered.

Bea was close on his heels, "Now what?"

"We check for a half-circle of stones just beyond it."

"Then we look for the grotto," Smidgeon reminded them as she caught up, gasping for breath. "This clinches it...I'm getting in better shape."

"Lance, do you think that's right?" Bea said, pointing toward an array of rocks ahead of them.

He surveyed the assortment of medium to large boulders that seemed to extend in an arc away from him in two directions.

"Yep, I'd say it's got to be it. Now, according to the notes, we go off this way," Lance said, pointing, and then he led the way up a small dry gully. "It should be up this arroyo."

About two hundred yards into the arroyo, the fading light illuminated a concave structure in the shallow canyon wall. "A combination of flash floods and landslides must have excavated that depression out."

"It's reminiscent of a grotto to me, or at least the shape of it is," Bea said. "But who knows if this is fifty years old or two hundred and fifty?"

"That's a good point," Lance said and he looked closely at the base. "It's sure weathered, so I am thinking it's been this way for a very long time."

Smidgeon added, "I'll take your word for it."

"It's got to be a hundred feet across," Lance said. "It would take a person a year of searching to find something buried along there."

"And it could be up in the cliff face, not necessarily along the bottom," Bea added.

Smidgeon wiped her brow and sat on a nearby boulder. "I guess that's why this penumbra thing is so important."

"Along with Holly," Bea reminded Smidgeon.

"Right. Poor Holly. I hope she's okay."

Lance said, "They'll take care of her until they get what they want."

He walked around, surveying the area. "We better see if we can find a place where we can hole up before it gets dark."

"If they're coming, they'll probably be along soon as well," Bea said.

"Oh, I have no doubt they're coming," Smidgeon said. "Nobody goes to this much trouble for nothing."

"Like us?"

"I don't care about the treasure," Smidgeon said, "but I do care about Holly. We're responsible for some of her trouble, so we have to get her back."

"Hey," Lance said, "she came to us."

"Yes, she did. But the way I see it, once we offered our help, we were committed to the whole deal."

Lance turned to Bea. "I still don't quite understand why you wanted to be a part of this."

"I'm intrigued by the story, and I was impressed by your willingness to help out complete strangers. I mean, Smidgeon, you had met Holly, what, just once before?"

"Yeah, just by chance."

"Yet she somehow found you out in her moment of need. There's something else at work here, and I think that is what made me curious. Besides, like I said before, I love a good caper."

Smidgeon laughed. "It *is* a caper, isn't it? Just like in some book."

Bea laughed and said, "Exactly."

Lance interrupted, "Enough chit-chat. We need to get out of sight. That bunch of scrub over there looks big enough. We'll be protected by the canyon wall on one side and it looks thick enough to hide us." He led Bea and Smidgeon over to the spot.

"We have a good view of the approach from here," Bea said.

Lance added, "And we should be concealed pretty well."

Smidgeon tried to lift a large rock. "It sure would be nice to have something to sit on."

Lance tested the weight. "Whew. You're right but it might take the both of us."

They struggled with one rock, then worked on another. Once it was placed next to the first one, she panted, "I need to take a break."

Bea said, "I could help with a third."

"They're pretty darned heavy, you sure?"

"If I move stacks of books around a library, I think I can help carry a boulder."

She squatted and grabbed a medium sized-rock, and grunted as she lifted with her legs. She awkwardly walked it over to the other two and carefully placed it on the ground.

"See?"

Smidgeon beamed. "Lordy, Bea!"

"You know, I do work out regularly," she said.

With this operation complete, Bea and Smidgeon crouched low behind the bushes as Lance walked off a couple of hundred feet, then returned slowly. "Looks really good," he said, "If I didn't know you were there, I probably wouldn't notice you, even in daylight. Could you see me okay?"

"Clear as a bell," Bea said. She pulled a small pair of binoculars out of her pack. "And I have these as well."

"Good!"

They settled into their lair and munched on crackers and water as the daylight began to gradually wear into dusk. Lance and Smidgeon made sure their guns were within easy reach.

~ * ~

Michaels took a swig from a canteen as he kept his eyes on Sam. "Do you think you can make it?"

"It's worse than I thought it would be. It's not an intense stabbing pain, but my leg is very sore."

Ximena sat quietly and stared at Sam before getting up and rubbing her hands together and placing them on his leg. "Here?" She closed her eyes, inhaling and exhaling very deeply.

"Yes," he said, then he stammered, "h-h-hey, what did you do?"

She blushed and smiled. "We must go now."

Michaels shouldered his pack, Sam limped behind him, and Ximena followed a few steps behind them, carrying her big bag like a sack of groceries.

"How's the leg?" Michaels called back to Sam.

"Better."

"I hope we don't just happen upon the bad guys. They might get the drop on us."

Sam panted. "This was the way Lance said he had scouted, so I think we'd have seen their car when we started, or we'd hear their car behind us. Of course, they could be following another trail."

"That's probably the case," Michaels said. "There are a lot of trails out here."

"I wish we had a third radio. Mule could warn us if they drove up."

"It's getting dark, so they must be hiking up there just like us. Are we sure we're going the right way?"

Ximena whispered, "Yes."

After another forty minutes on the trail, she held up a hand and said, "Stop."

She ran ahead of them about ten yards and crouched down, then turned back to them after they joined her, and very softly whispered, "We must be quiet. *They* are near."

"The bad guys?" Sam asked.

She nodded.

Michaels and Sam exchanged questioning glances as Ximena held up one palm as a hold signal, then swiftly motioned for them to advance a few yards, then they stopped again at her signal. In the distance they could see three figures. One of them was stumbling along between the other two.

"That's Holly in the middle," Sam whispered.

Ximena put her hand to Sam's mouth and turned to him, shaking her head. They heard talking. At first it was indistinct but in minutes they could hear bits and pieces of the conversation.

"Don't know why we had to come out here in the dark with no lights or nothing."

"Shut up, Ding, you know we don't want no one seeing. Especially with this girl all hog tied. Keep moving."

"Ya think we gonna be rich after tonight?"

"Whatever we find goes to Mendoza, but he'll give us a good cut. He promised."

"How's it supposed to work again?"

"Something to do with the moon and shadows. She's supposed to be the only one that can see it."

"See what?"

"I don't know. That's what we're supposed to find out when we get there."

"How we gonna dig up any treasure? We didn't bring no picks or shovels."

"I've got some stashed nearby. Came out a few weeks ago after we figured out where the girl was."

"Why'd we have to wait so long?"

"Something to do with the moon—it's happening tonight. That's all I know. Mendoza says it's starting about ten o'clock, so we need to move along."

Sam could see Holly struggling to keep up, bound and gagged. The three moved ahead, continuing where two trails merged into one.

When the voices faded, Ximena said in a very low tone, "Now we move...slowly and quietly. You now know how easily someone can be heard."

Michaels pulled out his service revolver and checked it, then holstered it. He nodded, and waved with the barrel of his other weapon for Sam to follow.

"I'm good," Sam whispered as he tightened his grip on the shotgun.

~ * ~

"It sure is dark. What time does the eclipse start?" Lance asked Bea.

"About ten."

"And what about this penumbra?"

"That's what starts the eclipse. There should be a penumbra after the full eclipse, too."

"Why is that?"

"I think it is the light outer part of the earth's shadow. There's a leading edge and a following edge."

Smidgeon stood up. "I need to stretch out my knees," and then she quickly crouched back down. "I think they're here! I saw a little movement and heard a voice."

"Yep, here they come," Lance whispered. "Looks like there are three of them."

"The one in the middle must be Holly," Smidgeon said.

"Yeah, I think so."

"Shhh," Bea said.

They began to detect snatches of conversation.

"Look, see? I told you I could find it." A pinpoint of light flashed back and forth. "There's the rocks, just like Rey said. Flat on one side, a circle on the other. And up this way is that little canyon he told us about."

"Get along," one voice said as he pushed the stumbling middle figure.

Lance could see Holly's hands were bound. The three dim forms were about thirty feet from them when Lance glanced at Bea and Smidgeon and nodded. Smidgeon grabbed her gun and Lance followed with his. He bobbed his head again and they quickly emerged with the two weapons trained on the group of three.

"Now you just stop right there."

Earl pointed his own gun at Lance. Ding had pulled out his own and held Holly close, pointing his gun at her head.

"Who's there?" Earl asked. "Drop them guns and come forward or we kill this little lady."

Smidgeon called out, "Let her go!"

"Best do as she says," Lance added. "We all know you ain't killing your ace in the hole."

"Well, you ain't getting her, we need her."

Smidgeon kept a steady aim at Ding. "So do *we*. She's our friend and we need her alive."

Earl took a tentative step forward. "You don't understand."

Lance retorted, "Stop right there! We understand everything. We know about the penumbra."

"Huh?"

"The moon," Bea said. "We know about the moon."

Earl glanced up at the full moon and his gun hand began to shake. "Maybe you do, maybe you don't."

"We know you are working for Rey Mendoza and we know about Holly and the treasure."

"It's not any of your business," Ding said, tightening his grip on Holly's arm. "None of this is any of your business."

"Looks like we have ourselves a good old-fashioned Mexican standoff," Earl chuckled. Then he stopped abruptly at the sound of a shotgun being racked behind him.

"Neither of you move. You know what they call a Mexican standoff in Mexico, Earl?"

"Who's there?"

"Do you?"

Ding was wild-eyed.

Earl managed a meek, "No."

Michaels chuckled, "It's just a standoff." He poked Earl in the shoulder with the barrel. "I'm a police officer. Earl Rector and Ding Stewart, you both are under arrest."

Sam jumped out of the dark, cocked his shotgun, and stuck it into Ding's back. The little man gasped and relaxed his grip on Holly, who broke free and fell away from him as he dropped his gun and ran off into the dark.

Earl called out, "Ding, you coward, stop and fight them."

"I don't think I can catch him," Sam said, looking back at Michaels.

Detective Michaels had disarmed Earl and was busy cuffing the burly criminal. "Let him go. We'll call Mule to watch for him."

Earl struggled against the handcuffs. "Wait, I know you, you're from Roswell. This ain't your jurisdiction."

"Yeah, well, maybe we'll be able to sort that out later. As for now, you're under arrest." Michaels proceeded with the standard Miranda warning routine.

Smidgeon went closer. "Sam! What are you doing here? You were supposed to stay back!" She hugged him and added, "I should be really mad at you, but I'm glad you're here. You were just in time."

"Ximena insisted I come with her and Detective Michaels."

Lance spoke up. "Ximena? Where is she?"

Sam looked around. "I don't know. She was right here."

Bea untied Holly's hands and Smidgeon removed her gag.

Holly coughed and retched for a moment. "Oh, my God," she said. "How did you ever find us?"

"We never gave up on you," Smidgeon said.

"When they grabbed me, I know they shot Dave. Is he okay?"

Smidgeon sighed deeply. "He didn't make it, honey. I'm so sorry."

Holly dropped to the ground and sobbed. Smidgeon crouched next to her and hugged her.

Bea looked up at the moon. "It's beginning."

Earl sobbed softly, "He'll kill me, he'll kill me."

"We'll sort that out later, too. You cooperate and we'll protect you."

"You don't know this guy. I'm dead, no matter what you do."

Holly shrieked, "I hope you all die for what you've done."

"What about your friend?" Sam asked.

Michaels prodded Earl. "Do you think Ding can find his way back down the trail in the dark?"

"I don't know. He's as dumb as a box of rocks, but he's also like a robot. If he has a notion in his head, he does what he's bound to do."

"Report back to Mendoza?"

"Yep."

Sam said to Lance, "Go ahead and call Mule on the walkie. We watched them come up a different trail on our right."

Lance interrupted. "Of course! I think there is another trailhead a mile east of where Mule is."

Holly composed herself and stood, still sniffling. "Mendoza is there. He brought us here in a black van. He has another man with him."

Lance talked into the radio. "We think they're parked at another trailhead east of you. Black van with two people. That Ding guy is headed that way, too, but we have his gun."

"I read you. I'll see what I can do. How's Holly?"

"We've got her; she's safe."

Earl spoke up. "What are you going to do with me? I'd prefer you just kill me. Just get it over with."

"Earl, what kind of punishment is that? You need to sweat it out for a few years before you're killed...for David Adams' murder."

"Wha...? That wasn't me. That was Mendoza! He was the one behind it."

"That's for the court to decide."

Holly screamed, "It was you who pulled the trigger, Earl. I saw you!" She looked up at the moon then sat on the ground again. "I feel...strange."

Smidgeon handed her a canteen. "It's just the shock of everything. Drink some water."

She took a sip, then said again, "I needed that, but it's not why I feel strange. I think it's this light. It's making me dizzy and giving me a headache."

Bea looked up at the moon again. "It's the penumbra; it's progressing. What do we want to do? Do we want her to look for this thing?"

"I guess I don't know what you are talking about," Michaels said.

"It's hard to explain," Sam said. "But we think it has everything to do with the Archangel Cache."

Michaels shook his head. "Sounds like crazy talk."

"It does," Lance said. "I think we owe it to Holly here to play this out, if it's what she wants to do. Seriously, it may never be over for her if we don't deal with this tonight, while we have the chance."

"Come!"

They all turned and saw Ximena standing in the center of the arroyo.

"It is time!"

"Ximena!" Lance started toward her but she held up her palm and pointed to Holly.

"She's pointing at me." Holly started forward. "I don't know why, but I know I have to go with her."

"Wait," Lance said as he took a step forward.

"No, Lance. Just Sam." Ximena said, waving them both forward.

Lance took another step and Ximena cried, "No, you must stay here!"

"I've got this, buddy," Sam said to Lance. "Stay here and watch out for everybody."

Smidgeon grabbed Sam's arm. "Sam, I'm very afraid...don't go."

He turned to look at Ximena then back at Smidgeon. "I'll be fine. It's shadows. We're looking for shadows. Stay here with Lance. I'll be back in a few minutes."

Sam joined Holly and once they were with Ximena, all three made their way up the arroyo.

"I have a bad feeling about this," Lance said.

"Me, too," Smidgeon said.

~ * ~

The deeper they went into the arroyo, the darker it seemed to get, despite the full moon.

"Penumbra," Ximena said, almost as if she were in a trance.

Holly wavered and Sam steadied her. "What do you mean?"

"From what we've been able to figure out," Sam said, looking up, "the penumbra is the beginning phase of an eclipse of the moon. There's something in the stories about the shadows. And here, with these shadows, you are supposed to be the only one who will see it, whatever it is."

"Why just us three?" Sam asked Ximena.

"I am here to protect you both as best as I can," she said. "She is here because of the penumbra and because he expects it."

"Who?"

"The evil one. The protector spirit."

"And why me?"

"*Your* protector requires it."

"My protector?"

"Yes. I don't fully understand, but this is what I feel and know."

"Sam?" Holly said suddenly.

"Yeah?"

"Over there. It's different." She was pointing just up the arroyo wall, in a deep shadowy depression carved out in the rock.

Ximena pointed. "*La Gruta.*"

"What?"

"She means grotto. It really *looks* like a grotto in this light. The shadows give an impression of fernlike plants everywhere."

Holly stood in silence, transfixed. Then she meekly uttered, "I see it."

"What?"

"The outline of...of...an..."

"What?"

"Angel...it looks like an angel with its wings spread out! Right there!" She screamed, pointing.

She took a few steps toward it when she was suddenly knocked off her feet.

Ximena reached into her bag and pulled out a crystal, then stepped forward, facing the cliff face. "Stop!" Her fists were clenched and her arms extended in front of her.

Sam blinked as something began to glow in front of them. Sam could make out bearded features and glowering eyes. The entity looked up as another glowing object materialized.

"Loot!"

Holly stood, transfixed. "I still see it, the angel, but I don't understand what is happening. What are they...are they fighting over it?"

"Not sure. But you need to tell me exactly where the shadow is pointing."

She waved vaguely toward the wall but details were obscured by the increasing glow of two spectral images who were locked in some kind of ghostly struggle.

"I'm going to try to get around them. I think I can make it. Wave when I'm at the right spot."

Holly nodded. Ximena stood in front of her, transfixed with her fists reaching out.

Sam made an arc around the concentrated radiance until he reached the canyon wall, then he proceeded, glancing back repeatedly until he saw Holly wave. He looked up at the wall and saw nothing. He looked around the base, bathed in the faint light, but all he saw were small rocks and scant scrubby vegetation. He pulled out his pocketknife and plunged it into the packed soil.

"That will have to do," he whispered. Then he looked up and saw the bearded figure watching him, still in a tight spectral embrace with Loot's presence. A sudden burst of brilliance caused the figure to turn back to Loot and the battle continued. Sam was afraid to move from his marked spot. He waved to Holly and she waved back. Suddenly Sam felt a force around his throat, lifting him off the ground and against the arroyo wall. Then, just as suddenly, the force seemed to lurch away from him and he fell to the ground. He twisted and tried to let his good leg take most of the force but he still felt a jolt in his bad leg.

Then the glow abruptly ceased and both entities were gone. Holly ran to him, and Ximena followed.

"Are you okay?"

"I think so. I managed to land on my good leg." He took a tentative step and winced. "Mostly."

Ximena joined them.

Sam glanced down at his knife sticking out of the dirt and thought, *That will have to do.*

They made their way up the arroyo and returned to the group, with Holly and Ximena helping Sam.

Smidgeon ran to him. "What happened? Did you hurt your leg?"

"I fell. I'll explain later. I'll be okay."

Earl pointed his chin at Ximena. "I don't want to be nowhere near that witch."

"On your feet!" Michaels said. "Don't worry, you'll be leading the way. She always brings up the rear."

Sam sat on the ground and rubbed his leg.

Lance stooped. "You okay, buddy?"

"I hope so. Took quite a bump."

"Did you see it?"

"I didn't see anything, but Holly sure did."

Smidgeon joined them. "I overheard you. We saw some sort of flickering light but that was all."

"It's hard to explain what happened, but Holly directed me, waved at me to stop, and I managed to mark the spot. Should be pretty close."

"Can you walk?" Smidgeon said. She was still holding her forty-five.

He got up and took a few steps.

Bea came over and felt around his leg. "It doesn't feel like anything is broken and it's not bleeding."

"Come on, honey," Smidgeon said as she swung his arm around her shoulder. She waved to the others to move out. "We'll be along," and she struggled with Sam behind the rest of the group.

"Can you go faster? I can't even see the others anymore."

Sam struggled. "I'll try."

"I told you not to come out here."

"I know. But I..."

A glow of light materialized around them and Sam was suddenly lifted into the air and tossed twenty feet.

"*Usted no es digno!*"

A hazy bearded figure hovered over Sam, who had collapsed in a heap.

In a panic, Smidgeon raised her gun at the figure.

Twenty-two

Mule navigated the narrow trail toward the graded road, then turned east as Lance had instructed. At a turnout about a mile down, he saw a black van with heavily tinted windows. Mule stopped and waited. One of his hands remained in plain view on top of the steering wheel, but the other hand rested on the gun he had tucked close to his leg.

The driver's door opened and a man emerged and approached. He was large, powerfully built, and his nose showed signs that it had suffered more than one break in the past.

The man asked, "Lost?"

"Maybe. Looks like you might be lost, too."

"I'm waiting for some friends out hiking. They're overdue but they should be along soon."

"So, it's just you in the van?" Mule impatiently tapped his fingers.

"I'm with my boss. Look, mister, why don't you just move on?"

The van's horn beeped twice.

"The boss wants to meet you."

Mule sucked his teeth. "Tell him I'm quite comfortable where I am. If he wants to meet me, he can come over here."

"He can't do that. He can't walk, so you need to get out and come meet him. Like now." The big guy pulled out a Glock and pointed it at Mule's head. The car horn beeped again and as the man's head momentarily turned, Mule moved his assailant's wrist away from his head and slammed it hard against the door frame. In another second, Mule had pulled his own gun around to point at the big man's head.

"Drop it."

The man's gun fell against Mule's shoulder. He opened his door and the gun dropped to the ground as he got out. He kicked it under his car.

"Now, put your hands behind your head and maybe we'll both go meet this so-called boss after all."

The passenger window lowered as they approached.

"Keep your hands behind your head and kneel at the car door with your feet crossed." Then he called to the window. "Let me see both your hands out the window."

Two hands appeared and the fingers wiggled. "I am not armed. You show the distinct mannerisms of a police officer. Are you?"

"Used to be. Sorry, I don't much like having guns pulled on me."

"I can empathize with you on that point, sir." The voice had an old-school refinement. "I see that you managed to disarm Nicholas quite handily. Might you let him up? It is difficult to find and train a new driver, and I would absolutely hate it if you accidentally blew his brains out all over my van. I just had it washed and waxed."

"Any more guns in there?"

"Just the one Nicholas was holding."

Mule didn't believe him. "You're Rey Mendoza?"

The man showed surprise at hearing his name but dipped his chin in a shallow nod. "Do I know you, sir?"

"Name's Mule Hollis."

"Ah, the private detective who has been nosing about. Mister Hollis, I assure you, there is nothing for you here. We are waiting for some friends who wanted to go hiking. It is a nice night for it, despite the lunar eclipse."

"I have friends out hiking as well."

Mendoza feigned surprise. "You do?"

"You can cut the BS. We know about the penumbra, we know about your daughter, and we know all about the Archangel Cache."

Mendoza raised one eyebrow and locked his eyes onto Mules. "Then you should also know I will stop at nothing to get it. It belongs to me."

Nicholas tried to grab Mule's gun, but he was off balance and fell flat on his face. Mule put a foot behind the big man's neck. "Try that again and you're going to get fired for ruining the paint job." Mule removed his foot. "Now, just stay down there with your hands behind your head."

"Perhaps we should all, me and my friends, and you and your friends...perhaps we should all try to work together. There is very likely enough for everyone."

"All we really came out here for was the girl. She had no part in this."

"But if you know everything, as you say, you know she had a very important part in this. That is why I have tracked her for years, and it is why when her boyfriend was conveniently incarcerated with two of my men, I had them seek him out and make friends with him. It was all part of a plan that I'm afraid has led us to this place and time. Sadly, I could perform her task, but I'm unable to, as you see." He patted his legs. "Even the best wheelchair in the world wouldn't get me up that trail."

"That's a shame. Of course you must know that my friends are out there, too."

"Do you think they are a match for my men?"

"They have been before."

"Ah, and I confess that I do not understand that incident. They blamed their failure on a small girl with magic powers. I'm afraid I don't believe in such things."

"I didn't used to."

"So this girl is out there as well?"

Mule said nothing.

"You are a resourceful man, Mr. Hollis. Perhaps I could entice you to come work for me. Obviously my vetting process has been lacking." He nodded toward the prone figure of Nicholas. "I would pay you handsomely. More than you could possibly imagine."

"I'm just here to get the girl."

The sound of a distant gunshot echoed in the night.

Mendoza's mouth twisted into a sneer. "I'm afraid she may no longer be part of the equation."

"Get up," Mule said to Nicholas. "Get in the car and drive off."

He got to his feet and Mule led him to the other side of the van where he got into the driver's seat.

"Face it, Mr. Hollis. She's dead. Your friends are probably dead as well."

"You face it, Mendoza, it might be one of your guys who's dead," Mule said before slamming the door, "and maybe both of them." He waved the car on and it sped away, leaving a cloud of dust.

Mule backed his car up a few feet, retrieved Nicholas' gun and put it under his seat. He picked up his radio.

"Lance, you there?"

"Yeah. We're fine. You okay?"

"I found Mendoza. We had a minor tussle but I chased him off. What was that shot I heard?"

"Um, slight, uh, complication, but everything's okay here. I'll explain when we see you."

~ * ~

The shot had echoed loudly through the surrounding countryside. Lance immediately turned and ran back to Smidgeon and Sam.

"What happened?" he gasped as he got to them. "I told Michaels to keep walking with Earl, and I ran back here."

"Something grabbed Sam."

"Was it Ding?"

"I'm okay, just give me a minute," Sam panted. "No, it wasn't Ding."

Smidgeon hugged Sam. "I didn't know what else to do so I took a shot."

Ximena was by his side.

Lance voiced surprise. "How'd you get here so fast?"

Her dark eyes glowed intensely as she looked up at Lance before she returned to Sam, placing her hands on his leg, then on his head.

"It returned, yes?"

"Yes, I think so."

Lance asked, "What returned?"

Sam swallowed hard. "De la Garza..."

"Wait, the dude from the stories? The padre...?"

Ximena touched Sam's chin, turning his face back to hers. "Did it speak to you?"

"Yeah, but I didn't understand it; it was in Spanish."

224

Smidgeon stood and said, "What I heard was something like, '*Usted no es digno!*'"

Ximena said, "It senses the other spirit's connection to you and thinks you are not worthy." She pulled a small cloth pouch from her bag, opened Sam's mouth, and put several pinches of powder on his tongue. "This will help."

She crooked her head toward the dimmed moon and said, "We must leave this place. It is still near its full power and we must get far away as fast as we can. The girl saw the vision, and you marked the spot of the thing it seeks to protect."

"Did you see it?"

"No, only she saw the vision. And while the evil one was fighting the other, she directed you to it."

"The other?" Smidgeon asked. "What other?"

"There is no time! We must go." Ximena helped Sam to his feet and pointed at Smidgeon. "This one broke its spell with her gun. Its power comes from the place you marked and it must have returned there."

Sam stood. "My leg feels better."

"It will last long enough for us to get far away," Ximena said, "before the vengeance begins."

Lance followed Ximena, "I just hope somebody can explain all of this."

"You and me both," Smidgeon said.

"There is no time!" Ximena repeated. "We must go now!" Ximena hurried down the trail.

~ * ~

In a short time, they met Mule and quickly made their way back to Capitan where they assembled in Mule's room at the motel. Sam rested on the bed with his leg elevated, and the rest of the group sat where they could on beds, chairs, and dressers.

Michaels said, "Okay, I will have a lot of explaining to do back in Roswell tomorrow, but Holly gave her statement and the county deputies took Earl into custody. They also told me Ding was picked up wandering along the same road where we parked."

Mule laughed. "He was probably confused because Mendoza wasn't there for the rendezvous."

"Right. Anyway, Ding is in custody as well." Michaels stretched and yawned. "Tell you what, I'm beat, but I'm going to head back to Roswell. It's been interesting." He turned to Mule. "If you want a job with us, I'll put in a word for you. There's still a lot of lawman left in you."

"Second job offer I've had tonight," Mule smiled. "Mendoza mentioned hiring me."

"I'll bet he did, and it's a good time, too, because he's definitely got a couple of openings." They both laughed. "Well, come see me on your way back so I can tie off the loose ends in my report."

"Fine, Fred. You did really good work tonight."

"I'm just glad Holly is safe and Earl and Ding are where they belong."

After Michaels left, Holly spoke up. "So where does that leave me?"

Mule turned to Bea. "When did you say the next eclipse is due?"

"October seventeenth."

"I'd say you are still in danger until Mendoza gets what he is after."

"What does that mean? Are you talking about what I saw?"

Sam said, "You're the only one besides Rey Mendoza who could possibly see it. As long as it is still out there, every time there is a lunar eclipse coming, he'll be looking for you because he can't see it for himself."

Smidgeon said, "You need to get as far away from here as you can."

"But won't I have to go testify or something? Those men roughed me up and held me prisoner."

"I imagine so," Mule said. "But I'll talk to Michaels about it. I'm sure we can get you the protection you need."

"There's another option," Sam said.

"What's that?" Holly asked.

Smidgeon put her hand on Sam's arm. "No, Sam."

He turned to her. "I wasn't thinking me!"

"What the heck are you two getting at?" Lance asked.

"It's simple. Someone has to go back and find the treasure."

"How are we supposed to do that? You mean where Ximena said you *marked* it?"

"Yes. Right, Ximena?"

Ximena stood. "Yes. She," she said pointing at Holly, "directed him and he placed a small knife on the spot. The other spirit fought the evil one while Sam did this."

"Wait," Lance said. "All these spirits! How many spirits are we talking about?"

"Out in the desert? Just the two," she said. "The ancient one and Sam's spirit."

All eyes turned to Sam and he sighed. "I think she means Loot. I don't know how, but it's Loot."

"Who the heck is Loot?" Mule asked.

"You're living in his house," Lance said. "He was Sam's partner in his gold mine days."

"Oh, the one who was murdered? I wish somebody had bothered to mention this earlier. I'm not sure I like the idea of living in a murder victim's house."

Holly said to Sam, "So you see ghosts?"

"Just the one, and not very often."

"This spirit is Sam's protector," Ximena said. "The other is evil, and the thieves' hoard it protects is the center of that evil."

Bea spoke up. "I don't know about the spirits, but if Sam marked the spot revealed to Holly during the penumbra, we might indeed be able to find it."

"But the evil," Ximena said.

"Didn't you say it had less power without the penumbra?" Sam asked.

"Less, yes, but…it still protects."

Sam turned to Ximena. "Can you help?"

"Perhaps."

"We'll need supplies," Sam said.

Smidgeon spoke up. "What's this we? You're staying right here."

"We may need his protector," Ximena said.

"I don't care. I am his protector on this side of the street."

"With you there, Ximena, maybe they'll be okay. Lance should be able to do anything that needs to be done."

"So what's the marker?"

"There's a depression in the right side of the canyon wall."

"I saw that when we scouted around before you got there."

"It's along the base of the wall a bit left of center in the depression. If you look there, you should see my knife jammed into the ground. It was the only thing I had."

Bea spoke up. "We'll need shovels and picks. A metal detector would be nice, but we'll already have plenty to carry."

"Salt," Ximena said. "Always salt. And Lance carries a special protection as well."

Sam said, "So did I…it didn't seem to help."

Ximena turned abruptly. "You are alive."

The comment caught Sam off-guard. "I guess you have a point there."

"The hoard is still evil," Ximena said.

"Perhaps if we had a noble purpose," Bea said.

"What do you mean?" Mule asked.

"If we find it, we turn it over. It wasn't Padre de la Garza's and it isn't ours. It either belongs to the Church, or to the government, since it is now on federal land. We turn it over."

"A noble cause is always the best cause," Sam said. "Besides, treasure is more about the finding than it is the spending."

Twenty-three

Lance pulled the car into the same spot they had parked in the previous day.

"Let's get the stuff," he said.

Smidgeon opened the back and pulled out a pick and a shovel. Bea and Lance pulled out the three packs. Ximena stood to the side, clutching her bag.

"I hope Sam is all right. I know I told him he couldn't come, but he wishes he could have joined us."

Lance said, "Dang, Smidgeon, last night I had to practically carry him the last quarter mile. Even *he* agreed he was in no shape to hike."

"I know."

"He'll be fine," Bea said. "But I sure wish we were getting an earlier start. I'd hate to be out there at night again."

"The evil one is more powerful at night."

"I'm with all of you. I'd like to be done before sunset, but the moon will still be mostly full," Lance said, "so we'll have some light if we run late."

Smidgeon hoisted the pick over her shoulder, "I don't want to wait to find out. Let's get going."

The four explorers walked single file down the trail and into the wilderness for the second time in two days.

As they approached the now familiar outcrops at the end of the arroyo, Bea said, "The second time seemed faster."

"It always does," Lance observed. "You're more mindful of details on the first trip...makes it seem longer." He looked at his watch. "But we really spent about the same amount of time on that trail."

"Anybody need a break?" Smidgeon asked.

"Do you?" Lance asked.

"Not me, I'm anxious to push on."

"Are we set on what we are going to do if we find anything?" Bea asked.

"It hurts me to say so," Lance said, "but I guess we're going to turn it over."

"I'll use my contacts with the university to find a suitable organization to inform."

Smidgeon said, "I just want to break this curse or whatever it is and let our lives get back to normal."

Ximena began walking up the arroyo. "We must keep going."

Once they reached the depression in the wall, Lance walked to the center and dropped his pack. "Now to look for Sam's knife."

He slowly scanned the base of the cliff, watching for anything that wasn't dirt, a rock, or a plant. Ximena joined him. In a few minutes, she stopped and pointed.

"*Aqui.*" She said.

Lance joined her. "The knife!"

Bea and Smidgeon had been searching along other parts of the cliff, and they quickly converged on the spot. Bea was brandishing a shovel and handed it to Lance.

"Shouldn't we start with the pick?" Smidgeon asked.

"I'll test it first."

"We don't want to damage anything," Bea reminded them.

"Wait," Ximena said. "The salt, where is it?"

"There's a five pound bag of it in my pack. You insisted so I brought it. What do we need it for?"

"Protection," she said as she hurried to Lance's pack. She returned with the bag, opened a corner of it and began to pour it in a wide semicircle around the small group. She threw handfuls of it against the cliff face as well. Only a few particles seemed to stick where she threw them; the rest tumbled to the base. She poured the remainder of the salt along the base.

She said, "This will have to do."

Lance got to work, but his progress was slow. He could only dig an inch or so each time he chipped the business end of the spade into the packed earth.

"If anything was buried here, it's had three hundred years of baking under the hot New Mexico sun to lock it in tight."

Smidgeon handed Lance the pick. "Here, Lance."

Bea said, "I suggest moving a little away from the cliff. It's a general location, but if anybody buried anything of any size here, they likely buried it away from the wall."

"Makes sense," he said as he moved a couple of feet away from the wall and started chipping at the ground with the pick. Smidgeon removed shovelfuls of debris as he continued hacking at the ground.

"Hope no rangers show up. We're probably not supposed to be doing this."

Bea laughed. "It's the other problem with a treasure like this. The federal government would likely lay claim to anything anybody might find."

Lance managed to hack a hole into the hard earth. "About eighteen inches down." He puffed. "I wonder how deep they would have buried anything."

"They wanted to hide it, so I imagine it's probably pretty deep," Bea said. "They likely had several people digging. Do you want me to try...to give you a rest?"

"Maybe in a little while; I'm okay for now," he said as he dislodged another few inches of dirt and stone. "Getting a little easier the further down I go."

Smidgeon and Bea took turns shoveling the material Lance loosened. The hole was about three feet across and two feet deep. Lance extended the sides of it by another couple of feet, then continued working down.

"Hot work," he said as he took a break to sip some water. Bea continued while he rested.

Bea swung the pick ferociously. "I'm missing my aerobics workout, but now I feel less guilty," she joked.

She gratefully handed the pick back to Lance and he said, "You're a hard worker; you done good."

"Thanks," she panted.

~ * ~

The spectral image of Loot floated invisibly just beyond the group working at the cliff face.

"Glad you joined me, Scamp," Loot told another shadowy figure. It was Lance's grandfather, Scamp Norton.

"How'd my grandson get all mixed up with three ladies? And where's Mister Sam?"

"I've been here before. I helped Sam by keeping another spook occupied while Sam found something."

"Another, you mean like us?"

"Stronger."

"That ain't good."

"Warn't nothing good about this one. This is why I called out to you. Glad you came."

"If it's to help my Lance, I'm here with you, Loot. I remember her," he said floating over Smidgeon. "We've watched her before, 'cause she was helping Mister Sam."

"Joe Toll's daughter."

"From that café. I remember, but who are these other two?"

"The younger one is some kind of conjurer." Ximena looked up at the sky as Loot said this. "See, she senses us, I'm sure of it."

"Good conjurer or bad conjurer?"

"Good...I think."

"And this spook, is he here, too?"

"Lurking, like us, but he's keeping himself hidden. He's wary of something; it's keeping him back."

"Us?"

"Maybe. Could be he's scared of the both of us."

"Who is it?"

"He's Spanish and he's old, that's all I know. And he's had a lot of years to work on his power. It was all I could do to hold him back for Sam to do what he needed to do. Then we both faded as our energy ran out."

"I ain't practiced it as much as you."

"If your loved ones are threatened, it comes to you all natural-like. It did for me. You still know Spanish?"

"A little. I picked it up working with *vaqueros*."

"Might come in handy."

~ * ~

Sam, Mule, and Holly were sitting in a booth at the motel's café.

"This waiting is awful," Holly said. "Why didn't we go out there with them? What if they need help?"

"Sam needs to rest his leg, and the two of us aren't up for all this hiking. How is your leg, Sam?"

Sam said, "I managed to hobble down here from our room, didn't I? Seriously, I think it's just real sore from too much effort. Icing has helped and it seems to be settling down. I think we need to just sit tight. They should be back before it gets too late."

"I hope so. I just want to put everything behind me." Holly began crying. "I haven't even had time to process what they did to Dave."

"Wish we could have done him more good," Mule said. "We started all of this to save him, and I'm afraid we didn't help him at all."

"And now we have to save ourselves," Sam added.

"And Mendoza, my so-called father. Where is he?"

Sam said, "You can bet he's not far off, but at least we've taken care of most of his gang."

Mule rubbed his eyes. "I wish that was the case. Something tells me he has reserves."

Sam added, "You're probably right."

"I made a big mistake when I confronted him," Mule said. "I told him we knew about the penumbra."

"Then he has to figure we might have found it. I mean, since Holly was with us."

"That's what I'm afraid of."

~ * ~

"Something shiny!" Lance said as he dropped to his knees. He began to scrape away loose pebbles and soil, then clawed at the clumps of dirt to reveal a smooth yellowish surface that reflected the sunlight back into his eyes.

"I think it's *gold*."

Bea and Smidgeon peered into the opening. "I see it," they both said in unison. Then Bea scouted the surrounding area until she found a short oblong piece of limestone with a crude point on one end and brought it to Lance.

"Use this like a small hand pick but be careful. Gently work it around the edges."

Lance handled the rock gingerly as he scraped away at the surrounding dirt that entombed the artifact. "This might just work."

He clawed at the object, trying to move it, then repeated his efforts as he scraped around the edges. "I think I'm getting it," he said.

"I wish we could all help," Smidgeon said.

"There's no room," Bea said.

Lance threw handfuls of loose dirt over the edge of the hole. He was kneeling in the three foot deep depression. "I think it's coming out!" He tugged hard then fell on his rear, holding a golden stemmed cup of some sort in his hands.

"It looks like a chalice! It's amazing," Bea said as Lance held it up. "Look at the workmanship!"

"There's got to be more," Smidgeon said.

Lance looked up from the hole. "Probably. But we've verified *something* is here. Do we keep digging or do we turn the site over to somebody official?"

"Put it down!" Ximena said as she reached into her bag and withdrew the same jewel she had used earlier. She stood, clenching her fists, and stared up the cliff face.

~ * ~

"Uh-oh, here he comes," Loot said, pointing.

Pebbles and dirt tumbled down the cliff as an ethereal force descended.

"Quick, Scamp, how do I say stop in Spanish?"

"Uh...*alto*, I think."

"*Alto!*"

The descent stopped and an image began to form. It hesitated, as if unsure how to proceed.

"Looks like some kinda preacher man to me. Old, like in picture books."

The figure glared at the assemblage below, then shifted its glare to Loot and Scamp. On the ground, the smallest figure held up her fist and a light seemed to be emanating from her hand and surrounding the four figures below.

"She's doing something," Scamp said.

"So am I," Loot said and he swooped at the figure. "I said *ALTO!*"

More rocks fell as the two entities grappled.

"*No prevalecerás!*"

"He says you can't beat him...I say it's time for two against one," Scamp said as he joined the fray.

"*Mi nieto!*" Scamp screamed as he tried to prevent the figure from reaching down into the glowing circle.

It screamed in frustration as Loot and Scamp renewed their effort to push it back up the cliff. More gravel filtered down as it disappeared from their view.

~ * ~

"What just happened?" Bea said, dusting off the smattering of pebbles and dirt from her hair and shoulders.

Ximena collapsed and Lance hurried to her side, cradling her in his arms. "Ximena, what was that?"

"The evil one returned. They stopped him."

"What do you mean, they stopped him?"

"Sam's spirit...and *yours*," she said, pointing at Lance. She closed her eyes and her head fell limp.

"Get some water, quick."

Smidgeon retrieved her canteen and Lance splashed some water in Ximena's face. Her eyelids fluttered and he lifted her head and dribbled a little water over her lips. She sucked at the liquid then opened her eyes.

"Lance?"

"I'm here, Ximena."

"We must go now. First fill the hole, then we must take the cup and go."

Bea was standing nearby. "I agree. We found what we're looking for. I don't know what that was all about, but I could feel something strange happening right over our heads."

"It was a battle between good and evil," Ximena said.

Lance said, "I don't know about that, but I felt it, too. It's late afternoon...we should be packing up anyway."

"Fill the hole," Ximena repeated.

"Right away," Lance said, as he tucked the golden object into his pack.

He began shoveling dirt and stones back into the hole. "Should be easier next time."

Smidgeon helped him, using the top edge of the pick to shove piles of debris over the edge like a push broom. "Hopefully there won't be a next time, at least for us. I have a bad feeling about this place."

"This cup has a special meaning to the evil one. More special than all the rest. This is why it was placed last."

"All the rest? There's more?"

"Yes." She pointed at Lance. "He is almost done," she said, "we must go before it gathers its power again."

"Need to mark the spot somehow," he said. He picked up the pick and scratched at the cliff face. "No, that's no good."

He looked around and found a boulder with a flat side about ten feet away. He used the pick's flat edge as a lever and found he could pivot the boulder. It was big and heavy, about two feet in diameter, but once he pivoted it, he managed to rock it and move it forward about two inches. He let it down.

"If you three help, we should be able to get this thing over the spot. Then if we can turn it flat side up, it will be a good marker."

Working together, they were able to move it much further on each pivot. Smidgeon and Bea took turns on the pick, and Lance hefted the stone a few times. When it was at the edge of the disturbed soil of the hole, both Smidgeon and Bea hefted the pick handle together and Lance joined with Ximena to roll the stone over. The flat side was on top.

"Well, it ain't level, but it doesn't need to be. I'd recognize it," he said as he brushed the surrounding soil around with his boot. "Gotta try to cover our tracks."

Ximena looked up again. "We must go now!"

They gathered their belongings and headed back to the trailhead.

Twenty-four

Sam answered a knock at his motel room door and saw Mule holding some well-used, but functional crutches.

"Where'd you get them?" Sam asked as he looked them over.

"The motel owner saw you hobbling from your room and wondered if you could use them. He said he found them in a room a while back and kept them."

Sam tested them. "This helps a lot. I should have thought to bring mine, but I've been getting along pretty well up to now."

"You hungry? Holly's gone over to the restaurant."

"I could do with a bite."

"Do you think you can make it on those or do you need me to drive you?"

"These feel pretty good, just my size. Let's walk."

Holly was nursing a cup of steaming coffee when they came in. "I'm glad to see those worked out for you."

"Yeah, at least I can get around better now."

"That's good," Holly said, as she stared at the swirls of vapor rising from her cup, "because I have an odd feeling."

Mule looked up from his menu. "What kind of feeling?"

"It's distressing, like something is gnawing at me from inside. I know it sounds crazy, but I think they might be in trouble and need our help."

"How could you know that?" Sam asked. "I mean, we're all worried about them but..."

"I don't know how, but I know we need to go back out there."

Mule sighed. "I generally deal in facts, but lately all I'm getting are *feelings* about this or that."

"If you don't want to take me, I'll just drive myself out there."

"Oh, I'll take you. Sam, are you up for a road trip?"

"Yeah. And I think it must be catching. I'm getting the same vibe."

The waitress came up. "What'll it be?"

"Three burgers all the way, fries, and three coffees," Mule said, adding, "To go."

Holly looked at him with a question in her eyes.

"A person's gotta eat," he said. "Trust me, we don't want to face trouble on an empty stomach. We'll head out to their trailhead just as soon as the food gets here and eat on the way. The truth be told, I'm a bit anxious myself."

"I like this plan," Sam said. "Mule, you go get your car and I'll pay, then we can get on the road."

~ * ~

"Lance is taking them back to their car," Scamp said. "Should we go after them?"

241

"I think we better stay here. I think he's going to follow them."

"What is this all about, Loot?"

"I don't rightly know...some fool thing Sam and that danged gal of his got themselves mixed up with..."

"I didn't see Sam."

"No, not this time out, but he was here last time. I reckon my helping her helps him somehow."

"Who's the other woman?"

"I have no idea, but she seems to be able to handle herself."

Loot looked up the cliff face. "I can sense some rumbling from up yonder...I reckon he's getting ready to pounce again."

"Don't worry about me; I'm ready."

A glow spread down the cliff and moved quickly toward the trail the three had taken.

"Here he comes! Let's get him," Loot said.

Three swirls of vapor collided, and in the approaching dusk they created a glow that cast shadows behind the nearby rocks. Dust swirled and small stones scattered.

"He's strong," Scamp said.

"There are two of us. Push."

The other figure mumbled in Spanish as it grappled with them in the growing twilight.

~ * ~

"What's that behind us," Bea said.

Lance stopped and looked back at the unnatural, devilish glow. "Can't be no good. Keep going."

Smidgeon had paused to look as well. "Why would there be a light back there?"

"We must move away from this place," Ximena urged. "Quickly."

Lance led the way. "We should hit that jeep trail soon. Then as soon as we get to Bea's car, we can get out of here."

They all heard trees splintering and cracking. Smidgeon looked behind them. "Whatever it is, it's getting closer."

"Could it be a bear?" Bea asked.

"A bear wouldn't be carrying a light," Smidgeon said. She tripped as she ran, falling to her hands and knees.

"You okay?" Lance had stopped and called back.

Ximena helped her stand. "She is fine, keep running."

They reached the jeep trail and ran down it until they saw Bea's car. Before they could get to it, a black van rushed up to them. Smidgeon lagged behind the other two. She looked behind her...she didn't see Ximena.

"What the..."

Before she could complete her sentence, the van stopped and the driver jumped out holding a gun.

Lance and Bea paused and stared.

"Stay right there," the man said.

Smidgeon came onto the scene and froze. The driver waved for her to join the other two. She glanced behind her but said nothing. She knew Ximena was behind her somewhere. The three of them silently stared at their captor.

A voice called from inside the van, "Bring them to me."

"Around there," the gunman said as he directed them to the passenger side of the vehicle.

They slowly walked around to the window.

The gunman ordered, "Drop your packs."

The door opened and the figure inside said, "You are out hiking late."

Lance whispered, "Rey Mendoza."

"Ah, you know me."

"I know of you."

"I don't believe I've had the pleasure."

"Lance. This is Bea and Smidgeon."

"Ah, Lance. I believe you were a recent guest of my associates."

"I was hardly a guest."

Mendoza chuckled, then a wave of recognition flashed across his face. "Wait! Smidgeon Toll? The famous café owner from Texas? I am honored."

"I wish I could say the same."

The driver rifled through their packs. Smidgeon hoped he wouldn't find her gun, but he stopped after pulling something from Lance's pack.

"Mister Mendoza, look at this," he said, handing a heavy object to his boss.

"Nicholas, you have done very well, my friend." Mendoza turned the chalice around in his hands. "Eighteenth century. Very nice." He looked up at Lance. "So, you seem to have found my treasure."

"Don't know what you're talking about."

"Come now, Lance. The time for subterfuge is over. We know you and your group were out here last night looking for the Archangel Cache. Your friend, the private detective, told me you all knew about the importance of the penumbra. My men failed me, but it is now obvious to me that you were successful."

"What's it to you?"

Mendoza chuckled. "Interesting comment. It is worth quite a lot to me, but far more than any monetary value. This is the legacy of my ancestors. *That* is why it is important to me."

"That's crazy."

Bea spoke up. "It is an archeological site on federal land. We're turning it all over to them."

Nicholas took a step toward her and raised his fist. "Shut up, you."

"Now, now, my dear Nicholas, it is not nice to hit a lady. But she has brought up an interesting point...if I am to reclaim my family's legacy, I can't very well have you telling the authorities, can I?"

Smidgeon stepped forward. "Go ahead and kill us. You'll never find it. There's something else you should know, too."

"What is that, my dear?"

"It's protected by an evil spirit."

Mendoza laughed again. "Really, now, an evil spirit?"

"The other woman who was with us last night told us. She's a *bruja*. We saw things, strange things, and tonight, something was following us."

"For heaven's sake..." Mendoza cradled the chalice in his lap. "Nicholas, place these three in their vehicle and dispose of them. Then put their packs next to the bodies and burn the car."

"Move, you three."

As they slowly walked to Bea's parked car, Smidgeon kept looking around, wondering where Ximena was. Then there was another sound of wood splintering very close. Nicholas looked toward the noise, and from the side of the unearthly glow, a small figure suddenly sprang forward and pushed him. He fell hard, dropping his weapon.

Ximena grabbed it and stood over him.

"Don't shoot me!"

Her eyes fixed on his as she aimed the barrel at his head.

Lance ran to her and took the gun. "I'll take over."

Nicholas blubbered, "I-I wasn't really going to kill you."

"Now why don't I believe you?" Lance kicked at his feet. "Get up!"

More sounds came from up the trail, this time very close.

"What is that?"

"Can't be nothing good," Lance answered. "Your boss, is he armed?"

Nicholas remained mute.

Lance motioned with the gun, "Is he?"

"He keeps a gun under the seat."

Smidgeon said, "Mine is in my pack. If I can sneak up there, I could maybe grab it..."

"No time," Lance said. "Grab the gun out of my boot and hold it on this guy. I'll try to catch Mendoza unawares and disarm him."

Smidgeon held Lance's gun on Nicholas. "One sound out of you and you're a dead man."

Nicholas nodded.

Lance walked nonchalantly to the passenger side of the van.

"Nicholas? I didn't hear any shots...wha...?"

Lance held his gun to the side of Mendoza's head, reached under the seat and withdrew the automatic he found there. He stuffed it in the back of his waistband.

"Now, I'll relieve you of this," Lance said, picking up the chalice. He looked up as Smidgeon and Bea marched Nicholas to join them.

As they approached, Nicholas pretended to stumble and swatted the gun out of Smidgeon's hand. He shoved her down and ran for the open driver's door.

This sudden action startled Lance, and Mendoza took advantage of the diversion to snatch the chalice from his hands.

Mendoza slammed his door and screamed to Nicholas, "Drive!"

As the henchman jammed his foot on the accelerator, the area was bathed in light.

Lance was sure he saw two sources of light, the first from the road, followed by one coming up the trail.

~ * ~

"Keep it up," Loot screamed. "We can't let him get to them."

"The closer he gets to them, the stronger he gets. I can't keep this up much longer."

"Me neither. I don't want to know what he might do if he catches up to them before we tucker out."

Trees splintered and rocks flew. As soon as they saw the two vehicles, Loot and Scamp faded as another light flashed across the scene.

~ * ~

Mule came around a turn and exclaimed, "There they are!" Then he added, "That's Mendoza's van!"

Holly gasped and put her hands to her head. "No! Why is my head pounding? It feels like it's about to explode. What's going on?"

Mule could see Lance holding a gun and then saw another man push Smidgeon down and run for the car. Then from the left, another light came up. Mule slammed on his brakes.

"What is that?" Sam said, then he realized, "Just like last night!" He grabbed his crutches and stumbled out of the car.

Mule and Holly joined him and they all hurried toward the scene as they saw Mendoza's van begin to move away in a swirl of dust and gravel. Holly rushed into the cloud of dust.

~ * ~

The figure of de la Garza, once free from Loot and Scamp, descended on the moving car, lifting it as the wheels spun furiously at thin air.

"Should we try again?" Scamp asked.

"Just wait," Loot said. He noticed a small figure with a glowing fist near his friends.

Then they both winced at a bright flash and saw a small object fly out of a hole that suddenly appeared in the roof of the car. The other spirit lunged after it as the car fell to the ground upside down, the wheels still spinning. Then one of the group, someone Loot did not recognize, picked up the prize and de la Garza stopped abruptly.

"No! *Uno digno*, no!" And his spirit faded.

"I'm not sure what he means."

"What did he say?"

"A worthy one," Scamp said. "The *vaqueros* would say that at a rodeo after they saw someone ride a really frightful horse."

~ * ~

Mule and Sam joined Lance, Smidgeon, and Bea. They were transfixed as they watched Mendoza's car rise into the air, fall, and burst into flames. Holly came out of the cloud of dust clutching something in her arms, holding it close to her chest.

"I saw this fly out of the car before it fell and I picked it up. What is it?"

Lance turned and gasped. "That's what we found out there! Mendoza had taken it from us."

"He was going to kill us," Smidgeon said, "until Ximena came up and saved us."

"Where is Ximena?" Lance asked.

Bea pointed off to the left and they all saw a small figure lying on the ground. "There!"

Lance ran to her. "Ximena!"

She reached up and took Lance's hand. "I am all right. The cup, does Holly have the cup?"

"Yes, she picked it up."

"And everyone is alive?"

"Yes, we're all fine."

"Help me up."

Lance lifted her to her feet. "It was you?"

"The evil one, it wanted that thing. The man in the car was evil, too, but I managed to push the cup out and away from him." She looked at Holly holding the chalice. "She is good and her goodness completes the circle of evil and good surrounding that thing. The evil one is gone."

"He is?"

"Your spirit protector fought well, as did Sam's. They earned us the time we needed."

She pulled Lance to her and he hugged her. "I want us to be together," she said.

"I want that, too. I-I think I love you."

She smiled. "It will not be an easy life for you."

Sam came over on his crutches. "Get a room, you two."

Ximena blushed. "Not until we are married."

Lance held her face in his hands. "Married?" She nodded.

They all turned toward the burning vehicle. The fire was almost out.

"I think we need to get out of here," Mule said. "Once we can get to a phone, I'll call it in as an accident." He scratched his chin and chuckled to himself. "Danged fool thing for them to do, speeding like that on a narrow dangerous road like this."

Lance and Bea grabbed their packs, and Bea handed Smidgeon her pack. "I agree with Mule," she said, "let's get out of here and head back to Texas."

Twenty-five

Several weeks later, Bea and Mule surprised Smidgeon as they came into the cafe together.

"Bea? I didn't know you were in town."

"I wanted to fill everyone in...a lot has happened."

"She dropped by my office on the way here," Mule added. He winked at Holly as she approached them. "Miss Holly."

"Hi, Mule, oh, and Bea! What a surprise!"

"You're still here?" Bea asked.

"Yeah, I don't really have any other place to go."

"I heard you may be Mendoza's only living heir."

"I know he was rich and all, but it's all dirty money."

"Probably not all...but money is money," Mule said.

Sam and Lance came out of the kitchen.

"Oh, I didn't know there was going to be a party," Sam joked.

"Bea wants to give us an update."

Lance looked around. "What about Ximena?"

A voice came from behind. "I am here."

They all spun around.

"Where'd you come from?"

"Manny, the cook, let me in." She smiled. "He owed me a favor."

"It's almost closing time, Sam, flip the sign. I'll let Manny go."

Holly said, "Let him stay and finish his work, I was going to give him a ride."

Bea turned to Sam and asked, "So your leg is better?"

"I just asked too much of it. Getting thrown to the ground a couple of times didn't help."

"What helped was another week of walking on your crutches," Lance said.

They pushed two tables together and all settled in.

"Thanks for coming," Bea started. "It will be announced very soon that 'hikers,' meaning us, stumbled across an artifact that revealed what researchers think is the fabled Saint Michael the Archangel Cache."

"We already know that. What did you do?" Lance said.

"I drove to Albuquerque and met with the Laboratory of Anthropology at the Museum of New Mexico."

"Those are the people you had me lead out to the spot," Lance said.

"Correct."

"Why did you go to them and not the feds?" Sam asked.

"Well, they were better suited to assess the historical implications and coordinate if need be. The chalice has been authenticated as an eighteenth century artifact. The initial reports from the dig site indicate some amazing finds, all dating back to the correct period. There are many unique pieces. This is a good thing that will further our understanding of the Spanish colonial period in New Mexico and the New World."

"In short," Mule said, "we couldn't have gotten away with keeping it for ourselves anyway."

Bea laughed. "Probably not. Oh, I'm sure there are unscrupulous collectors out there who would have paid a pretty penny for some of those things, but you have to find such buyers, and by even asking around, the word would eventually get out and alert the authorities. Raiding archeological sites is a pretty serious crime."

"So they know you were involved and they know Lance was involved."

"Yes. We've asked to remain anonymous."

"Did anyone tie this back to Mendoza's wreck?"

"Not that I know of."

Mule screeched his chair back. "I can answer that. No. I touched base with Fred Michaels in Roswell and from what he could find out, it was seen as a one car accident caused by speeding."

"Not entirely untrue," Lance said. "He *was* speeding away with his supposed prize."

"I just wish Dave hadn't..." Holly began to sob. Smidgeon got up and hugged her.

"You just go ahead and cry, honey."

Sam said, "It's ironic, we only got involved to save him, but that was the one thing we couldn't do."

"Who knew we'd find so much trouble?" Lance said.

"What about these two," Mule said, waving at Lance and Ximena.

Bea laughed. "That's right. Mule tells me congratulations are in order. Have you set a date?"

"Next month," Lance said. "Priest couldn't set it up any time sooner because of details. I've been baptized, but now I have to study up."

"Oh, to be confirmed," Sam said.

"Yeah. I've been lax about church-going since I've been out here. No better time than now to get back to it," he said, holding up Ximena's hand and kissing it. "Of course I have to unlearn my heathen Baptist ways."

Ximena blushed, then spoke. "I am sorry I did not fully understand the evil we were facing, but from what she," Ximena pointed at Bea, "has told us, it was a very old spirit who could not let go of his connection to the treasure. He was very powerful. We very well might have died."

"We have you to thank for that," Lance said.

"No, I did what I could, but it was too powerful for me. It was your protector...and Sam's."

"Oh, dear. I've had enough of this talk about spirits," Smidgeon said.

"And she," Ximena added pointing at Holly. "She had a connection to the treasure as well, and when she picked up the golden object, the spell of evil was broken because, unlike the other man, she is a good person."

"So Holly saved us all," Sam said.

"Yes. The evil would have hounded us all if she had not broken the spell."

"And now, I guess we have a wedding to plan," Smidgeon said.

Ximena beamed, and blushed again.

"There is more news," Bea said. "I'm moving here."

Sam had been leaning back in his chair and he dropped it to the floor as he leaned forward. "What?"

"I'm going to work with Mule."

"Wait a minute..." Lance said.

"Don't worry, I'd already planned on moving out. I figure once you two get hitched, I'll just be in the way," Mule said. "I'll be renting a new place with an office as soon as I can find the right space."

Bea added, "I decided I am just ready for a change. You have all shown me that my skills are just as valuable outside the academic world. I've got enough years to qualify for my pension, so I'm ready to move on, and Mule can definitely use my help. Given the experiences we've all shared, I know it will be an interesting challenge. I plan on getting my license, too."

"I've tried to tell her it's mostly chasing down philandering spouses."

"I'll take my chances," she said, laughing. "Besides, cheaters deserve to get caught."

Holly spoke up. "I've got news, too. I think I'm pregnant with Dave's child."

A stunned silence was interrupted by Bea, "That's amazing news, Holly, congratulations!"

Smidgeon stood. "I'm just..." she sat again and exhaled. "I'm just plain speechless. Well, of course, congratulations!"

They all joined in the chorus of happy exclamations, but in a dark corner of the dining room, Sam detected a familiar face hovering. He quietly nodded toward it and the figure smiled and faded from his view.

Meet Thomas Fenske

Thomas Fenske currently lives in North Carolina but he was born and raised in Texas, and his native Texan roots run deep.

He's braved long stretches of endless Texas highways in search of the best chicken-fried steak, chili, Texas BBQ, and Tex-Mex food. He's hiked west Texas mountains, canoed rapids on the Guadalupe River, suffered through waves of mosquitoes in The Big Thicket, and rafted the Rio Grande. He's blistered in the heat of the long Texas summers, endured hurricanes, ice storms, hail, wind, and floods. He has even ridden across ranchland looking for a lost "little doggie"...how many Texans can say they have done that?

Why did he leave the Lone Star State? Well, one must do many strange things to better provide for a family.

He and his lovely wife of thirty-plus years currently share their home with a dog and nine cats. Somehow, he still manages to write amidst the chaos.

Works From The Pen Of Thomas Fenske

The Fever

In the late 1800s, Ben Sublett was already known for his secret gold mine in the far reaches of west Texas. When Ben died in 1892, it was thought his secret died with him. Eighty years later in a central Texas jail, a dying, homeless wino named "Slim" Longo whispered a long-held family secret to twenty year old Sam Milton.

A Curse That Bites Deep

After years of frustration and sacrifice, Sam Milton's life seems to be on track. In The Fever he got the girl, he found the mine, and he hopes he'll soon have the gold, but he forgot one minor detail: the curse and its ripples are affecting almost everyone around him.

Lucky Strike

A bitter, decades-old grudge surfaces with a vengeance in a small west Texas town.

Penumbra –

Reluctant treasure hunter Sam Milton and his girlfriend Smidgeon Toll find themselves immersed in the search for a missing man they have never met and end up on the trail of a cache of ancient gold in the desert southwest.

The Hag Rider

This Civil War memoir explores a fifteen-year-old cavalryman's transition to manhood, complicated by the spectral manipulations of a hoodoo witch sworn to protect him.

Harmon Creek –

When political candidate Earl Swanger ended up stabbed and dead next to a bridge in rural Texas it looked like a case of homicide, right? Then why was it ruled an accident within two days? This fictional account revisits the 1930 cold case and the possible skullduggery behind the coverup.